FUGITIVES OF LOVE

What Reviewers Say About
Lisa Girolami's Work

Love on Location is…"An explosive and romantic story set in the world of movies."—*Diva Direct*

"The women of *Run to Me* are multi-dimensional and the running metaphor is well placed throughout this tale. Girolami has given us an entertaining story that makes us think—about relationships, about running away, and about what we want to run to in our lives."—*Just About Write*

Run to Me is… "An intense romantic story where love seems to be a lethal word."—*Diva Direct*

In *The Pleasure Set*…"Girolami has done a wonderful job portraying the wealthy dilettantes along with the complex characters of Laney and Sandrine. Her villain is a great combination of brains and ruthlessness. Of course, the sex scenes are fabulous. This novel is a great blend of sex, romance, and mystery, and the cover is perfect."—*Just About Write*

"[*Jane Doe*] is one of those quiet books that ends up getting under your skin. The story flowed with the ease of a slow-moving river. All in all a well-written story with an unusual setting, and well worth the read."—*Lambda Literary Foundation*

Visit us at www.boldstrokesbooks.com

By the Author

Love on Location

Run to Me

The Pleasure Set

Jane Doe

Fugitives of Love

FUGITIVES OF LOVE

by
Lisa Girolami

2012

FUGITIVES OF LOVE

ISBN 10: 1-60282-595-5
ISBN 13: 978-1-60282-595-6

THIS TRADE PAPERBACK ORIGINAL IS PUBLISHED BY
BOLD STROKES BOOKS, INC.
P.O. BOX 249
VALLEY FALLS, NY 12185

FIRST EDITION: FEBRUARY 2012

CREDITS
EDITOR: SHELLEY THRASHER
PRODUCTION DESIGN: SUSAN RAMUNDO
COVER DESIGN BY SHERI (GRAPHICARTIST2020@HOTMAIL.COM)
COVER PHOTO BY LISA GIROLAMI

Acknowledgments

My most humble thanks to Shelley Thrasher, my editor and teacher.

To Sandy Thornton, the Comma Queen, thank you for keeping those small little marks in line.

Carsen Taite, thank you for your law expertise and the chats on the phone when you should have been working.

A big huzzah to the entire BSB staff. All of you are my heroes and heroines.

And, for my readers, a most heartfelt thanks to each and every one of you.

Dedication

For Susan, the woman who makes me laugh so much I cry.

CHAPTER ONE

The wind blew onshore that day. It didn't much matter to Sinclair Grady because she could do her collecting whether the breezes blew on- or offshore. But as she looked up and surveyed the cumulonimbus clouds growing in dark mass and density, she sensed a sea-breeze front forming. That meant possible thunderstorms and, depending on how quickly the nor'easter developed, less time to gather the pieces she needed to finish her latest stained-glass window.

Sinclair had hiked out just after low tide that morning to search the crevices of the boulders that made up most of the beach. Her favorite spot, the rocky point closest to the southern end of a grouping of white spruce, hadn't produced much sea glass so far.

Yesterday, the satchel that hung from her belt was full. It had been a great day, which might have contributed to the fact that she'd found only these few pieces of white and green glass that currently made up her booty.

About two hours into her hunt, Sinclair climbed onto a rocky ledge that cantilevered over the turbulent sea and sat down. The pegmatite rock formation was chillingly damp and cold. Lately, her heart felt the same way: dampened, inhospitable, and not at all comfortable.

She gazed out over the expanse of frigid, gray water. A lobster boat circled slowly around the buoy of a trap. Its lone inhabitant shut off the engine and reached for the bright red-and-white buoy with his rope hook.

Though she sold only an average of one art piece a month, she would never call herself a starving artist. Each stained-glass window was a one-of-a-kind design, set with rare and valuable pieces of glass tumbled from the sea. The designs, depending on who interpreted them, evoked emotions ranging from poignant and moving to profound and stirring.

Sinclair never agreed or contradicted the buyer's emotional assertions because all of those feelings, and more, came from deep inside her. The emotions flowed through her hands as she toiled every night creating her art.

One enthusiastic buyer had recently commented that the deep blues and greens of her purchase suggested the excitement of a new life starting.

But no matter how much sea glass Sinclair collected and no matter how many stained-glass windows she built from the treasured jewels that washed up from the sea, she doubted that observation accurately assessed her work. Constructing a new life for herself seemed impossible.

❖

"Twenty days until opening night and we're looking really good," Brenna Wright said as she and her team busily catalogued paintings and sculptures for the gallery's new show.

Six staffers hung artwork and painted pedestals for sculptures while Brenna surveyed the three exhibit rooms, inhaling the fresh smell of new paint. They would cover the front desk in the first room with a tabletop on opening night, for the hors d'oeuvres and wine. Most of the people would congregate there. Since the exhibition consisted of more paintings than other media, they would hang in the first and second rooms. The back room would house the sculptures and other mixed-media pieces. Each room had movable box walls to allow for more display space and a few stylish chairs for contemplation.

All the walls were stark white, illuminated with cable and halogen track-lighting systems. The concrete floor had been stained dark red, and the ceiling was black to control light bounce.

She loved the commotion and excitement when her team fired on all cylinders toward one fruitful goal. "Lucy, how's the RSVP list coming?"

Lucy clicked through a few screens on her laptop. "Just about a full house. Three hundred and sixty-seven confirmed so far."

"Brilliant. You're the best assistant ever."

"Your popularity and this gallery's success made it happen, but I'll still take the compliment."

The upcoming show, titled From the Hand of the Artist, featured not only the works of Manhattan's best talent, but personal stories from all of them about their specific experiences while creating their art. The placards, placed just under each work of art, spoke about channeling certain muses or the unconscious flow from brain to brush. The artists also credited dreams, arguments, epiphanies, love, and angst-ridden rumination for their creations.

All the artists would speak about their artwork, which always elevated sales tremendously. Buyers loved to rub elbows with artists, and hearing them describe their personal inspirations heightened the excitement that caused wallets to spring open with increased frequency.

And that would be another coup for her. The competition, especially the Shanks Gallery, would be envious again. She thought constantly about staying ahead of her rivals and would do just about anything to deny them profits and fill her pockets.

Standing in front of a framed watercolor, Brenna said, "Carl, you'll remember to take the glass out of this frame, won't you?" The reflection told her that she needed to cut her brunette hair. The scissor-cut styling had almost grown out. And she could see most of her five-foot-eight frame, which meant the painting had to hang higher.

"I'll do that when I change the hanger," Carl, Brenna's assistant curator, said. "It's too low."

"Read my mind."

"And we still need the Leone piece. She's already sent us three of them but she still has the last one. I have the measurements but need to place it correctly with the other paintings in the back gallery."

"I'm going over there tonight to pick it up."

"Personally?"

Brenna drew her answer out to end dubiously. "Yes."

Carl stared at her with his usual pixie-like pursed lips.

Brenna frowned. "Don't make me ask why."

"Don't make me state the obvious."

"Nina isn't a factor."

"Nina's always a factor. I swear she cranks out paintings just so she can see you."

"She can see me anytime she wants. All she has to do is come down here to the gallery."

"Which she does. A lot. And you'd better cover that tattooed arm of yours. I hear she's a wildcat when it comes to body ink."

"Carl," Lucy said, "Nina isn't Brenna's type. Lay off."

"*Lay* would be the operative word, yes."

Lucy harrumphed. "That's all you think about."

"And Brenna doesn't think about it enough."

Brenna shook her head in annoyance. "Carl, more hanging, less talking."

CHAPTER TWO

It was just after one o'clock and Brenna was stuck in traffic, as usual. On her way over to Nina Leone's SoHo loft, she thought about Carl's comments. He was right that she didn't consider relationships often. Sure, she went out with women every once in a while. Some were even interesting enough to take home. But they rarely saw each other for more than a night or two only. Was she just too picky? Of course, when she took women to her parents' house, one certain look from her mother would always remind her of the devastating consequences of her first, and only, real girlfriend. She had to be extremely selective. Picky or not, she felt lonelier with the women she met than when she wasn't dating.

She simply never felt fulfilled, whatever that meant. And if she didn't know, maybe she'd never achieve that satisfying contentment or whatever it was that never seemed to materialize.

She knew what satisfaction in her career felt like. Just after she graduated from Columbia University's arts-administration program, her parents had financed her gallery and Brenna began work in earnest. Because of a senior-year internship in Paris, she named her exhibit and sales space L'Art de Vie, the art of life. She had initially shown and sold the artwork of her college peers, launching many lucrative careers while building her business into a multimillion-dollar enterprise.

Along the way she'd weathered some dips in the economy, and her parents backed her financially from time to time to float the staff and keep them in electricity. But Brenna had been single-minded in her efforts, especially after almost losing her business because of the serious slip in judgment that was her last girlfriend. Since then she'd spent every waking moment culling through magazines and the Internet, scouting artists and networking with those who could further her business.

Now well-known artists and agents solicited her for exhibitions, and she hadn't had a slow quarter in the last six years. Success came easily. People said her parents' bankroll had caused it, but no one doubted her workhorse ethics. She was often accused of being spoiled and not accepting no for an answer, but while she hadn't struggled like most of her college friends, she loved what she did and was extremely determined. Selling art was just as exciting for her as it was for the artist who created it.

Her love life, on the other hand, was far from fulfilling. L'Art de Vie nourished her and provided everything she could ever want, except a complementary and loving relationship.

❖

Sinclair selected a coveted piece of cobalt-blue sea glass as the centerpiece for the window on her work bench. From there, she would lay in lighter-blue pieces of glass for the surrounding areas, working the pattern out toward the edges where foamy white and light-aqua pieces completed the design.

She chose to work to a mix of Elton John songs from the seventies. She loved the melodies, and the works created the same calming ambience she had so desperately turned to as a child.

The rain came down rather insistently, starting with sporadic tapping on her roof, like polite requests to enter. But the growing storm quickly took on the characteristics of a nor'easter, developing into great wind gusts that shook her house. The clouds darkened abruptly, and the pattering of rain suddenly transformed into loud reverberations above her, like powerful applause from an enthusiastic concert hall.

She took a break and walked over to the French doors that led out onto the back deck of her home. Even through the sheets of rain, the ocean looked spectacular from there, a view she couldn't have afforded anywhere else. But in this secluded part of Maine, along a coast not conducive to sunbathing, let alone comfortable picnics for the tourists that congregated mostly to the south, land proved much more affordable. With public beaches like Popham Beach State Park in Phippsburg available, tourists didn't care to venture out to the sizeable and sometimes sharp rocks that made up her backyard.

That's why she'd picked Pemaquid Point. She didn't want anyone looking into her home from the shore, and she especially didn't want to make it easy for anyone to find her. Yet she fervently wished that she hadn't had to take those measures.

Sinclair inhaled deeply, trying to release the unrelenting slab of sorrow wedged inside her and exhale it into the atmosphere, away from her. She blew out her breath until she emptied her lungs and paused. But the anguish hadn't budged.

A small squirrel scurried through the downpour to her door. He stood up at the glass, attempting to look in.

Sinclair laughed and scooped up a peanut from a bowl on her kitchen table. She opened the door a crack and knelt down. With one hand, she pushed her long, curly blond hair away from her face and reached out with her other, holding the peanut between her finger and thumb.

"Hello again, Petey," she said.

His tail twitched with a mix of excitement and caution as he guardedly and jerkily stepped closer. He then opened his mouth and took the peanut. He stepped a few feet away and rested on his back legs, quickly shelling the nut with his teeth, chewing rapidly and devouring his snack.

"You don't care about the rain, do you, little guy?"

Her only nearby neighbor finished the nut and came back for another, and she marveled at how gingerly he accepted it. If the storm kept up, he absolutely would care about the rain so she grabbed a handful of peanuts and deposited them just outside her door. Petey froze mid-chew, seeming to assess his good fortune, then resumed chewing.

As far as this storm went, she would weather its onslaught, and if she was lucky, the first low tide might provide a jackpot of tumbled sea glass.

❖

SoHo wasn't the safest neighborhood in New York, but Nina had lived there alone for the past twenty years and, at night, Brenna always found a parking spot close by.

Nina buzzed her up and she climbed the stairs to the third-floor loft. Nina waited for her in the open doorway and took her hand, leading her into the large expanse of the loft. Her whole place consisted of only one room with a large working space filled with easels and taboret carts and smaller areas delineated by throw rugs to separate the kitchen from a sitting room and her sleeping area.

Nina's paintings adorned the walls in virtually every area and were spectacular. Her plein-air paintings, flush with the natural lighting that denoted that style of modern art, enriched the space in beautiful earthy tones.

"Let's have a drink," Nina said, and led her to a mid-century modern couch. The minimalist furniture presented a stark contrast to her art, but somehow, the mix worked.

"Only a quick one. I've got to get back to the gallery soon." Brenna stood while Nina poured something caramel brown into two glasses.

"Oh, nonsense. I'm sure it took you longer to get here than one drink would take. Relax, your curator won't take advantage of you while you're gone."

No, but you might, she thought. "One, Nina. You don't want me transporting your art while I'm banjaxed."

"I can always lend you another one."

Brenna had the feeling that getting out of Nina's place with only the painting would be more difficult than she thought. Carl was right. Again.

Nina handed her a glass. "A little bourbon."

Brenna sat down on the low-slung, red couch that looked more like three marshmallows laid on their sides and held together by chrome piping. It was more comfortable than she anticipated.

Again, she surveyed the room, taking in Nina's paintings. Then, hung in front of one of the windows that faced the street below, another piece of art struck her more powerfully than the plein-air pieces.

"Whose is that?"

Nina sat down next to her. "I just bought it. Don't you love it? I got it in Maine."

"Who's the artist?"

"Her name is Sinclair Grady."

"Where in Maine?"

"A little gallery called Breakers in New Harbor. They told me she was local. I rarely stop at those galleries. I mean, if you've seen one amateur seascape, you've seen too many. But that piece was hanging in the front window, and I've never seen one like it before."

Neither had Brenna. The individual pieces of glass weren't the normal sizes that most stained-glass windows were made of, but much smaller, and the pattern was like a wonderfully subdued but colorful mosaic of a radiating nautilus. Sure, she'd seen brilliant displays of beautiful stained glass, but this artist poured into her work the kind of passion that only the best oil painters could express.

"Those are pieces of sea glass," Nina said.

"From the ocean?"

"Authentic sea glass. Rare, too."

"Astounding." She gazed at the way the sun illuminated the art. She'd never felt so much emotion from stained glass. An intense sense of forlornness and separation overcame her. The solitary composition of the nautilus somehow revealed an intimate heaviness and vulnerability.

"I'm..." Brenna searched for the best word, "thunderstruck."

"I like how the true artist comes out of you when you're excited about a piece."

Brenna looked away from the window. "That's one of the most unique pieces of artwork I've seen in a long time."

"Are you getting bored with me already?"

"Of course not, Nina. Just wait for the opening of From the Hand of the Artist. You'll be the belle of the ball."

"Will you be my date?"

"Nina, I'll be there but it won't be a date. You know we've already had this conversation."

"Yes, yes. I'm not your type or some such drivel. But I don't plan to give up that easily."

"Nina—"

"Can't we just date a little? I've got such a crush on you. And I know you're not attracted to the shy type."

"What makes you say that?"

"I know the women you date." She counted off on the fingers of one hand. "They're artists, they're beautiful, they're mysterious, and they need lots of attention."

"And you're going to say that describes you to a tee."

"Doesn't it?"

"There's much more to it than that."

"You also date women who state their desires directly."

All those things were true, but so far that combination hadn't proved too successful. She certainly didn't want to date someone who was introverted and antisocial, but someone in between had to exist.

Brenna sipped her drink a little quicker because the conversation wasn't going anywhere. Just like the possibility of the two of them being together.

She looked back at the window. She had to find that artist. Hopefully no one else represented her. An exhibition of her work would be a smash hit in Manhattan.

Chapter Three

S he doesn't have a phone?" Brenna looked up at Lucy, who sat at the gallery's front desk.

"Nope. Not a listing anywhere. I've been on the computer for almost an hour. Her name doesn't come up at all on the Internet."

That could be a real coup for Brenna, since she seemed to be the first one to pursue the seemingly unknown artist. But she wouldn't be anonymous for long.

"How else can we find her?"

"I'm not sure. It looks hopeless."

Brenna pointed her finger upward, punching the air decisively. "Never give up. There's got to be a way."

"Did Nina meet the artist?"

"No, she bought the piece at a small gallery." Brenna smiled. "Nina said the place is called Breakers and it's in New Harbor. She said the artist was a local."

"They should know where to find her."

"I need to do this quickly. Shanks Gallery might have seen it too, and I'm going to get to this artist before they do."

"Our big bad boss has spoken," Lucy said, smiling.

"Carl." A wave of promise washed over Brenna. "I'll be taking a couple of days off to travel up to Maine. Can you handle the installation for a while?"

Carl stood with his back to her, his head tilted to the right, surveying the placement of three paintings for the Hands exhibit.

"That's what you pay me for."

"Good. Lucy, can you book me a room up there somewhere, please?"

"You're going without a solid plan. What if she's not there? What if you hit a dead end?"

She pointed her finger back up and Lucy cut her off. "I know, never give up."

Brenna could make the drive in eight or nine hours. It was better than flying because she could bring back some pieces in her car. If she spent two nights there, she could find this Sinclair Grady, contract her for a show, and be back in Manhattan before the bagels in her favorite bakery cooled down.

She felt the immediate thrill of a new discovery. While she spent most of her time negotiating shows with established artists, every once in a while she located fresh talent. Some with raw and original things to say in their paintings, sculptures, and mixed media, colored with the raw passion of love, struggle, or political opinion. Many provoked ardent critiques, some positive and some odious, but both types of assessments usually made their way to the nation's leading newspapers and online forums.

Brenna loved provocative shows, where the art would enrage some. And with just as much enthusiasm, she sought out shows that portrayed groundbreaking and innovative new forms of artistic expression.

Sinclair Grady fell firmly into the latter.

Collectors and critics alike were hungry for anything original. The freshness of the offerings seemed to act as a rush of oxygenated blood that would clean out their systems of the same old seen-it-before cookie-cutter phases that the art world was prone to fall in to.

When one artist's work exploded in sales, scores of others would flood the market with similar pieces. Brenna didn't dislike the deluge these trends caused; she profited very well. Certainly without periods of like-art, the world wouldn't have seen the beauty of Neoclassicism, the surprise of Surrealism, or the open composition of Impressionism. Mankind expressed religion, politics, and the human element through each of these periods, one influencing the next. Each era was extremely significant, and each variation within it could be exhilarating and valuable.

It seemed that the current movement remained stuck in a sort of relational art period where human relations and their social context influenced the art, and although the scene was full of versatility and vibrancy, it was also heavy with political commentary.

Sinclair's work, however, with its purity of shape and color, as well as the beauty of profound emotion, manifested an innovative and fresh artistic expression.

"I know that look." Lucy was staring at her. "You've found someone special."

"I haven't exactly found her yet, but yes, she has potential."

"New Harbor has a few places to stay. I'll book you a room. When are you leaving?"

A buzz of energy coursed through her at this new prospect. Her lungs filled with expectation and her fingers tingled with restlessness. Tomorrow's trip would prove that she'd made a memorable decision.

❖

Sinclair stopped by the Seaside Stop, the local bar in Pemaquid Point. She'd collected supplies and food on her once-a-week trip into town and wanted to have a drink and a chat with Donna, her ex.

The bar celebrated a life at sea, with nautical instruments and seafaring paintings decorating the walls. A dim, golden light glowed from ships' lanterns hung throughout, while music played softly in the background.

A television, hung over the small seating area, played a silent game of football, and the only other patrons, an elderly couple, watched and drank from large schooners of cold beer.

"Hello, Mr. and Mrs. Bellamy. Nice to see you."

"It's good to be seen, Sinclair. How are you?" the elderly man said while his wife smiled broadly.

"Doing well. Did you survive the nor'easter?"

"Was but a small spit compared to other storms."

Sinclair chuckled and made her way to the bar.

"Hermy has arrived."

Sinclair sat on a bar stool, its back wrapped in weathered rope. She ran a hand across the bar top, feeling the cool smoothness of the lacquer that had been applied as generously as on a ship's trim. "You know I don't like that nickname, Donna. I'm not a hermit."

"Sorry, honey. Old habits, as they say." Donna towered over Sinclair. Her still-strong high-school-basketball legs were clad in black jeans, and she wore a green T-shirt emblazoned with the Seaside Stop logo. "But it's not far from the truth, you know."

"That's why I come in here, Donna. I don't get enough nagging at home."

"Missed me, didn't you?" Donna smiled as wide as a Cheshire cat.

"Actually, I did."

"Whiskey?"

"Please." She watched Donna pour a shot, and when she handed it to her, she said, "I've sold a few windows recently." She tilted her head back and shot half of the whiskey, which made her close her eyes and purse her lips. "Nice," she said, after blowing out a stout breath.

"That's great. Looks like you'll be flush with heating oil for a while."

"Better than that. Two went to Los Angeles and one to New York, from what Kay said."

Kay ran Breakers, the gallery that sold her art. She chirped with excitement every time someone bought one of Sinclair's pieces. She lovingly supported the local artists and Sinclair's sales were increasing.

"Well, I'm happy for you."

Sinclair drank the rest of her whiskey, closed her eyes again, and shook her head. "Man, that's gonna warm my toes."

When she opened her eyes, Donna was watching her with an expression that Sinclair recognized. "I suppose now you're going to ask me if I'm happy."

"Something like that."

Sinclair didn't answer so Donna said, "Well, are you? Happy, I mean?"

"Compared to what?"

"Compared…" she said, the side of her mouth curling up in what looked like frustration. "My lord, Sinclair, you've always been a difficult one. Compared to as happy as you want to be, of course."

That was a tricky question. What did that mean—as happy as she wanted to be? She could imagine what being as rich as she could be was like. She could also imagine what being as rested as she could be felt like. But happy? What did she have to compare it to?

Donna lifted the whiskey bottle but Sinclair put her hand up. "Water, please?"

While Donna reached for another glass, she said, "I was happy when we were dating."

"Well, that's nice to hear. Especially since we remained friends afterward." She handed her the water.

"And I'm grateful we're friends. Do you know that?"

"I do, sweetie. That's why I'm asking you how you are."

"Does your wife know you've hung a therapy shingle?"

"She says it comes with the bartender's towel. Seriously, tell me how you are."

"I'm fine. But you're starting to worry me. What's this all about?"

"You."

"Well, I know it's gotta be about me since the Bellamys are too busy watching football."

"Sinclair, listen to me. You're one of the most wonderful women I've ever met. You're an amazing artist with more talent than pretty much any other oil-paint splasher or clay thrower around these artsy-fartsy parts. And that wide, bright Irish smile of yours can melt the polar ice cap. You're a catch, honey. Still, I worry about you."

"What's to worry about?" But she knew. And what Donna said next was pretty much word for word what she understood about herself and just couldn't remedy.

"You've lived alone for two decades and you're only thirty-five years old. Yes, we dated for a little while, and I was crazy about you."

"I was crazy about you, too."

"And I know you wouldn't allow yourself to go...deeper with me. I could see it in your eyes, honey, but you just wouldn't. Couldn't, I suppose. Do you know what I'm saying?"

Sinclair did know.

"And it's okay that it didn't work out. And since then, you've been out with a couple of others around town, but that's it. And I know you want more than that. You're capable of so much love, Sinclair. I know that for a fact."

She did, but what could she do about it? It wasn't that she didn't think about that very same subject herself, but when she did, nothing better than sadness and frustration came from it. And then she'd have to make a huge effort to shoo the uncomfortable feelings away with a swift, rain-soaked walk by the water or a log-splitting session out back, behind her house.

"Well, I think I've dated all three available women in town and Mrs. Bellamy is taken, so I'm back to square one."

"You could widen your circle."

"Why are you bringing this up, Donna? You're stating the obvious about my life. I don't choose to live in some bustling metropolis where I'm sure the girls dance four deep at the bars. I like my calm, quiet life here. I've got calm with no dates, okay?"

"I'm just saying that you could have both. A lot of people come through town, you know. You miss most of them because you're way off the beaten path, but they pretty much all stop by here."

"I know your intentions are good, Donna. But I'm fine, I really am." Sinclair stood and deposited a ten-dollar bill on the bar. "And I've gotta run along."

"I apologize," Donna said. "I'm being nosy. And I know you won't tolerate that."

"No, you aren't." And she wasn't, actually. All those people who came through town, however, they could be nosy.

That's what she couldn't tolerate.

CHAPTER FOUR

Turning off Highway 1 at Damariscotta, Maine, Brenna drove south along route 130 toward the village of New Harbor in the Pemaquid Peninsula. She tapped a beat of hopeful anticipation, knowing that within the hour, she would have Sinclair's address and, with a bit of luck, would be speaking with the artist.

Breakers Gallery, just past Indian Trail Road, was housed in a two-story board-and-batten house with weathered yellow paint and light-blue trim.

A stained-glass piece that had to be Sinclair's hung in the front window. It featured a magnificent tree overlooking the ocean with green and yellow glass and foamy white accents highlighting the blue water. Brenna's pulse quickened as it would if she'd spotted a gold vein in the old gold-panning days.

Inside, four or five tourists wandered around, looking at paintings and photographs, but with her tunnel vision Brenna saw only their blurry features as she searched out the owner.

"Are you Kay?"

A slightly plump woman in her mid-fifties looked up from organizing a countertop display. "Yes, I am."

"Hi. My name is Brenna Wright and Nina Leone sent me. She purchased a Sinclair Grady piece a while back."

"Yes, I remember her. From New York, right?"

"Yes. And I noticed you have another one of her windows."

"Would you like to see it?"

"I'd like to buy it."

Kay's face lit up. "Well, that's great! It's my last one. I've been pestering Sinclair to bring more in and now she'll just have to."

Brenna helped Kay retrieve the two-by-three-foot window, which proved quite heavy. As Kay wrote up the purchase, Brenna said, "I'd like to meet Sinclair. Do you have her address?"

Kay paused, her pen stopping its forward motion. Looking up she said, "She's not that crazy about visitors."

"Really?"

"She's the sweetest girl but keeps to herself mostly."

"I'd like to talk to her about showing her artwork in my gallery in New York."

"That sounds very exciting."

Brenna knew not to be pushy, but she hadn't come this far to be turned away. "I think her pieces are fantastic, and I believe an exhibition would do very well. So could you tell me where she lives?"

Kay hesitated. "I suppose it wouldn't hurt."

She helped Brenna carry the window out to her car and provided directions. "If you go down the road a few more miles, you'll turn right on Bristol and then make a left on Pemaquid Loop. When you get to a yellow mailbox on the right, go down that gravel road, but go slow because you may see some wild turkeys."

"Yellow mailbox, wild turkeys. I've got it. Thank you, Kay."

"She doesn't like surprises, so don't say I didn't warn you."

Turning at the yellow mailbox, Brenna rolled the window down and a fresh, salty breeze filled her car. Living in New York afforded her many aromas, but most were the smells of ethnic restaurants, exhaust, and damp concrete. Her wheels crunched on the gravel road, and she watched for wild turkeys but didn't spot any. An opening appeared through the trees, and she could see light-gray fog enveloping a white clapboard house.

She parked close to the front door and got out to take in the panorama. The expanse of ocean stunned her. From the bluff right behind her house, Sinclair had a hundred-and-eighty-degree view with no other houses close by.

The wooden steps to the front door creaked as if they were tired. Not seeing a doorbell she knocked. No sounds came from inside, or at least none louder than the waves crashing against the rocks below.

After a few minutes, Brenna walked around to the back of the house. French doors and large, wide windows revealed a beautifully decorated interior. The design was simple and efficient, with light-blue and white walls and a kitchen space that overflowed into the living room. An informal collection of teak and bamboo furniture looked very inviting and large, and a bookcase, overstuffed with mostly hardbacks and a few paperbacks, sat under a sizeable brass tide clock that hung from the wall. A light-blue wicker rocking chair faced one window, which Brenna imagined would be the perfect spot for contemplating the hypnotic roll of the ocean over coffee or tea. Speaking of coffee, it had been hours since her last indulgence on the road. Her nerves were beginning to jangle, and she really didn't want be on edge when she faced a potential client.

After knocking on the French door, she realized no one was home.

She turned around to watch the waves while she contemplated her next move. Sinclair could be in town buying groceries or art supplies, for all she knew. Heck, she could even be on vacation, which would lengthen her wait time quite a bit.

It was nearing dusk since the drive north had taken a large portion of the day. She supposed she could check into her hotel and wait until morning. But first, she wanted to take a quick walk to the sparkling water, which was light years superior to the Hudson River.

Climbing down the bluff's staircase, she realized that getting to the water would be more difficult than she'd thought. Large boulders looked as if they had been poured out of God's big bucket and tumbled in gargantuan piles between the bluff and the ocean.

There was no sand to speak of, which left the waves to break more dramatically against the boulders. Every few seconds, salt water spewed up in misty clouds and sea gulls gracefully veered one way or another to avoid them.

Brenna climbed over a number of rocks and stopped halfway to the waterline. She looked around her and marveled at the geology of the beach. Of the few things she remembered from science class, she identified the rocks as granite. And if her science teacher was correct in saying that the name came from large mineral grains that fit tightly together, her immediate vicinity consisted of a gazillion, million grains.

Dramatic streaks of white and black granite reached toward the sea as if trying to move in that direction. Crabs skittered in and out of the crevices, and empty lobster traps and fishing floats, in bright yellows and reds, littered the rocks and sand.

To the south, the rocks were darker and more jagged as they made their way to the point which, Brenna presumed, was Pemaquid Point.

She turned back toward the north to see a lone figure emerging from a small bend about a hundred yards down the coast. Even in the fading light, the shape was definitely female. Her movements were very fluid as she maneuvered around the rocks with the agility and familiarity of a local.

Was this Sinclair? Not many others lived this far out, and a tourist probably wouldn't be out there alone.

Brenna climbed back to the staircase, thinking it would be a better meeting place than the slippery rocks.

She waited for the woman to approach, watching her study the rocks as she hiked over them. Every so often, she'd stop and bend down to pick something up and inspect it. She placed several things in a satchel at her waist instead of the sack she carried.

As she neared, Brenna could see that the woman was close to her own age and very attractive. When Kay had said that Sinclair didn't like visitors, Brenna imagined a salty old woman, sallow from years of reclusion, with time bending her forward in a cantankerous curve.

But the person walking toward her was beautiful and nimble, maybe five foot five, with a slender build and curly, golden-blond hair pulled back in a baseball cap. Her ponytail had swung over one shoulder and rested there like an ingot sparkling in the last remnants of the sun's light. Her shorts revealed strong legs whose muscles reacted to each stride. Her broad shoulders looked as if she could carry a swimmer, fireman style, from the clutches of the ocean.

A feeling, stronger than anything she'd ever experienced, suddenly washed over Brenna. She was immediately drawn to the woman walking toward her, and the attraction hit her with a potent mix of magnetism and desire. She wanted her, but the power of the unexpected pull perplexed Brenna.

She didn't even know her, but it was as if the woman was returning to her—to her life and her arms.

The sound of the sea receded to a muffled rumble but her vision sharpened. If she were staring at an angel, she wouldn't be any more overwhelmed.

She lifted her hand to her chest because her heart began to respond to this strange experience with thumping urgency.

When the woman was about twenty yards away she looked up and noticed Brenna. She paused slightly, which concerned Brenna, who'd begun to wonder whether she was single or if she liked romantic little bistros. Then the woman was upon her.

"May I help you?"

The voice was more probing than inquisitive, and if her green eyes hadn't made Brenna clutch just then, the words would have.

"Hi, my name is Brenna Wright and I—"

"Are you lost?" The woman stepped past her and walked up the stairs.

Brenna followed. "No…I came here to…are you Sinclair Grady?"

When the woman stopped suddenly and turned, Brenna almost ran into her.

"What do you want?"

Brenna hesitated, her desires and fantasies suddenly slapped from her brain. The capricious bubble burst and she was back to reality, standing in front of a five-foot-plus vessel of rudeness.

"I said, what do you want?"

She was used to having artists eager to secure an exhibition in her gallery solicit her, not encountering unpleasant people who didn't give her the benefit of the doubt.

"I just bought a Sinclair Grady window." She quickly pointed to her car and thankfully the bubble wrapping showed above the front seat. "I own a gallery in New York, and I'm very interested in showing your work. Or the artist's work." Was this the artist? The artist's daughter?

The woman, who still hadn't confirmed her identity, studied her for what seemed like an hour before saying, "What's the name of the gallery?"

"L'Art de Vie."

Her eyes bore into Brenna's and, though they smoldered, their effect was far from anything she might fantasize about.

"I'll be back."

Stunned, Brenna watched the woman step onto the back balcony of the white clapboard house, walk inside, and close the door.

A cool breeze blew into Brenna's open mouth and she quickly clamped her lips together. While she hadn't assumed that the woman would be the Welcome Wagon, the borderline insolence shocked her. Yes, she had arrived unannounced, but how else could she find out about Sinclair? The artist didn't have a phone that she knew of. She hadn't even gotten a real address, just a yellow mailbox and some invisible turkeys.

Her mood dimmed and the thought of being left to stand outside prickled. Just screw her, she thought. I don't need this from a country newbie. She looked away from the house and shook her head. This could be a waste of a long drive.

Why did she have to be bad-mannered? Brenna was used to her share of obstinate creative types; however, the talent never merited the attitude. No matter how successful someone became, they never had a license to be a donkey's ass.

She scanned the yard and then looked at her car. The bubble-wrapped window in the backseat made her pause. The work was spectacular and truly original. And probably unrepresented. The impetus to remain where she was proved strong. However, she was also curious to find out if the woman from the beach was Sinclair or someone else. The artist or the daughter, discourteous or not, she might be the key to obtaining the art.

The possibility of a new and exciting exhibit made her refocus her thoughts

I need this acquisition. Never give up.

The French door finally opened and the woman said, "You can come in."

CHAPTER FIVE

K eep your own attitude in check, Brenna thought. Coffee or not, there was no need for two snarky people in this conversation. She smiled as she wiped off her feet and stepped inside.

"I'm Sinclair Grady," the woman said, and held out her hand. "I needed to check the Internet and confirm who you are. You've got a lot of photos posted."

"I produce a lot of exhibits." Brenna took her hand and nodded toward the computer. "Have a lot of art-dealer imposters visited you out here or something?"

"One can never be too careful."

Brenna wasn't convinced that her answer was completely truthful. She reached into her pocket and retrieved a business card. "Looks like you've already been to my Web site, but take this anyway."

Sinclair placed it on her table without looking at it. "So, you were saying before?"

"Yes. I'm interested in showing your work at my gallery. More than showing, actually. I'd like to create an exhibition. I'm fortunate to have a rather extensive following. Art dealers, buyers, and such make my gallery a regular stop in their art pursuits." She felt a bit awkward standing in the middle of the room. If she wasn't being invited to sit down, her time might be short so she'd have to talk quickly.

"You'll find a list of our past exhibitions on the site. We've shown important works at L'Art de Vie and many artists have gotten their start there. Some are so popular now, their prices have quadrupled and more. What I mean to say is that we're a heavyweight gallery with some serious chops. And now I'm interested in you."

Sinclair didn't respond right away. It was as if she were analyzing every word Brenna had spoken.

Was she not only mean but a little slow as well?

Sinclair removed her baseball cap and blond hair fell about her shoulders. Unquestionably, she was attractive. Her cheeks were pink from the wind and her eyes, though vigilant and suspicious, were the green of rough-cut emeralds.

She turned away, toward a diminutive kitchen just off the main room.

Brenna scanned the room and focused on the bookcase she'd seen through the window. The titles were impressive, with subjects ranging from art history to philosophy and economics to quantum physics. Her selection indicated that while Sinclair might be mean, she certainly wasn't slow.

"I'm making some coffee," Sinclair said from the kitchen. "Would you like some?"

The heavens were opening up. "I'd love some."

The woman standing on the rocks had startled Sinclair. Days would go by without seeing another human, and usually the ones she did see were out in lobster boats just offshore. Her chest seized when she realized the woman wasn't just a beachcomber who'd wandered too far off the beaten path, but someone looking for her.

She knew she'd been rude when they first met, but even the slightest indifference or carelessness could be hazardous. Still, looking up on her trek home to see an astonishing-looking woman standing by her steps had taken her breath away. Brenna was taller than she was and dressed in a light-green sweater and linen pants that didn't do much to hide the shape of her long legs. The sea breezes played magnificently with her thick brown hair, tossing it about her shoulders. She stood there looking very self-assured and resolute, and Sinclair had almost completely dropped her guard.

"Why my work?" Sinclair asked when she returned with two steaming mugs and invited Brenna to sit at the kitchen table.

"No one's ever asked me that question. Most artists challenge me with 'why not'?"

Brenna took a sip, and Sinclair wondered if her special clove-and-cinnamon blend had caused her slight smile.

"Because, Sinclair, it's unique. Because it evokes feeling. Because they're one-of-a-kind pieces."

She seemed sincere. "How does an exhibition work?"

Brenna laid her hand on the table and Sinclair studied her graceful fingers. A ripple of desire fluttered in her chest and she shook her head to expel it.

"We procure..." Brenna paused, staring quizzically at Sinclair. "We procure your work. That is, you loan us the work." Brenna picked her hands up and moved them gracefully through the air to emphasize her words. Sinclair forced herself to ignore the temptation again.

"We exhibit it at my gallery in Manhattan and take care of everything. That includes the cost of shipping, the exhibition, opening night, all staff costs. It goes on and on.

"You set the prices and we take a fee. Now, I must tell you that if you've never exhibited, the fee may appear high, but we're making a huge investment in you, and most of our fee covers our costs."

Brenna opened her hands upward as if offering her something very special and delicate.

Sinclair raised her eyes to meet Brenna's, which were chestnut brown. Their peaceful expression bumped up against her uncertainty. She detected no pretenses, no tricks.

"You love what you do," Sinclair said.

"Ah...ah..." Brenna stuttered.

Brenna suddenly seemed transfixed. In that moment, she was saying something with her eyes but Sinclair couldn't read it. It had to be important because her gaze was solidly concentrated, which worried Sinclair. Was she wrong about there being no tricks?

She closed her hands together as if she was now protecting whatever she'd offered. Her smile came slowly and genuinely as she responded to Sinclair's observation about her attitude toward her work. "I do."

Sinclair nodded, relieved and satisfied. "What's the fee?"

"The standard gallery fee is fifty percent. We take forty percent."

"That does seem high."

"Including the expenses I mentioned before, plus rent, insurance, and especially advertising, an exhibition costs around $10,000. We'd need to sell $20,000 to break even. But we create interest and develop a market. Based on the first exhibition, another one is scheduled within twelve or eighteen months. By then, the hype has usually spread and those who didn't or weren't able to obtain one of your works will jump on the popularity wagon. At least, that's why we invest all this time and money. And it's worked well for me so far. That's why I can charge less than fifty percent."

"But if I just sell a piece or two at Breakers each month, I'm very happy with the amount I pocket, which is considerably more than fifty percent."

"I understand that. And it's definitely your choice. But I'm offering an opportunity to branch out and become very much in demand."

"I'm not sure if I can produce pieces much faster than I do now."

"It's not so much about quantity, Sinclair. This type of exposure allows you to charge more, based on demand. An exhibition could increase that demand. People wait months for artwork from some of the best-known artists. Having few pieces can make the existing ones even more desirable." She looked at Sinclair, her face sincere and her words earnest. "I know you could charge four or five times what I paid for the one in my car."

"That would buy a lot of supplies."

Brenna laughed and Sinclair couldn't help but join her.

"Yes, that's a lot of soldering wire."

"Have you made stained glass?"

"No. But I've been around a little. I can speak linseed oil and Damar varnish with the best of them."

Sinclair liked this woman. She was intelligent and direct. And she seemed genuinely interested in her artwork. Her shoulders relaxed and she took her first deep breath since seeing Brenna on the beach.

"Maybe we could talk about an exhibition, then."

"That's fantastic. Thank you, really."

Brenna seemed delighted. She looked outside.

A dark-purple haze descended on the rocks. Soon it would be too dark to see the waves and all that would be left was their continuous roar.

"It's getting late," Brenna said, "so is it all right if I come back tomorrow? We have lots of things to talk about, and I'd like to see the rest of your work."

Sinclair needed to get to bed soon because low tide would come the next morning at 5:35. Spending more time with Brenna would be nice, considering she didn't get to socialize that much. Though the confusing feelings she had for a woman she hardly knew might be risky, she really wanted to see her again.

"How early can you get back here?"

"Early, ah, what would be good for you?"

"How's six a.m.?" Sinclair said, thankful that, other than identifying her as an artist, Brenna didn't know who she was.

CHAPTER SIX

Only chickens and Wall Street brokers got up this early, Brenna thought as her feet hit the cold floor on her way to the bathroom. She shivered and swore while she ran the shower as hot as she could. Lucy had booked her at the Pine Cottages, just off Route 130. The place was as quaint as the name, but she wondered if it was as old as the evergreens that surrounded it. Everything from the floorboards to the bed creaked as if too tired to take on one more tenant. The hotel's pipes groaned a little, but soon enough the shower was steamy and she was fully awake.

It had rained quite hard the night before. She stayed awake until close to one listening to a grand concert of thunder and lightning. By morning, the storm had passed and nothing was left but a lot of wet trees and puddles.

A place called the Seaside Stop, which looked like a bar and grill, sat across the street so she walked over to see if they had coffee. Her nerve receptors were calling out for some badly needed caffeine, and she'd eat the grounds from a spoon if nothing was brewing yet. The place was dark and the sign said they'd open at 6:00. It was 5:45.

"Shit," she muttered, looking around the small, darkened town. "The things I do to be competitive."

She didn't want to be late so she drove around to see if she could find anywhere else to get a java fix. Why had Sinclair chosen such a wretched hour to meet?

She had to admit, however, that she was glad to witness the Earth start a new day since she was usually asleep at this hour. The scenery was absolutely beautiful as she headed toward Pemaquid Point, and though she found absolutely nothing open at that time in the morning, the low-lying fog that hung on the road and the trees that dripped with moisture as the breaking dawn started to illuminate the flannel-gray sky deflected her craving for caffeine just a touch.

She turned at the yellow mailbox and squinted toward a few hazy blobs in the middle of the road. The blobs jumped, making jerky motions as they began to scramble, and Brenna recognized the wild turkeys she'd been warned about. She slowed down but the turkeys had no appreciation since they'd already disappeared into the brush.

The lights glowed amber in Sinclair's home as she got out of her car. The thick aroma of pine trees and salty air refreshed her and she felt encouraged. A thin swirl of smoke rose from the chimney, making the place look like a welcoming cottage. Beyond the wet, ebony rocks of the coastline, the vast ocean was blue-gray as far as she could see. The scene was as charming as any storybook location she'd ever imagined, exuding warmth, romance, and enchantment.

Sinclair opened the door and completed the picture as she looked radiant silhouetted against the glow from inside. She wore tan hiking shorts, a baby-blue sweatshirt, all-terrain tennis shoes, and short wool socks. She looked better than any model Brenna had ever seen in an outdoor-clothing catalogue. She recalled the day before when Sinclair had said, "You love what you do," and her expression had been so intense and filled with, what? Hope? Brenna had been immediately thunderstruck, unable to respond.

The green in Sinclair's eyes had sparkled and the look of suspicion had vanished. Brenna's chest felt heavy again and her mind went blank. Was she entangled in the storybook tale about a beautiful enchantress who spent her time casting spells on strangers?

"Good morning," Sinclair said, and stepped aside for Brenna to enter.

"I'll take your word for it that it's morning. I rarely see this dark time of day." Brenna paused, then said, "And I've never smelled coffee so inviting."

Sinclair smiled. "Let me pour you a mug."

Brenna wanted to kneel for communion, hold out her hands and accept the caffeine bullion. And when she took her first sip, she closed her eyes and moaned.

Brenna opened her eyes to see Sinclair's lovely, amused face. "Should I leave you two alone for a while?" she said.

"You may have to. It tastes even better than it smells."

"It's organic and was roasted yesterday."

"Yesterday? What cloud in heaven did this fall from?"

Sinclair shook her head. "Secrets stay tight in Pemaquid Point. That is, unless you talk to Sally at the local market, who roasts the beans. She's not too humble about her coffee mastery."

"I'll be clearing the shelves on my way back to New York."

Sinclair watched her drink, but when she asked her why she didn't have a mug for herself, Sinclair said, "I've already had two. And you'd better hurry up with that one. The tide's coming back in."

"We're going out?"

"You can see my work later. Right now I need to get more sea glass, and the best time is after the low tide. And the first low tide after a storm like the one we just had is the best." She hooked a satchel to her waist and said, "Come on."

Brenna took a big gulp of coffee, whispered lovingly, "I'll be back, my friend," and followed Sinclair outside.

They walked over slick, algae-covered boulders and reached an area where the rocks were quite small and large areas of sand had been deposited.

Sinclair scanned the ground the entire time, constantly searching the rocks and sand around her.

"Tell me your process. Is the sea glass just…out there?"

"The motion of the water and sand over several years and even decades will naturally tumble any glass that finds its way to the ocean. Low tide is the best time to search since material is deposited as the tide recedes. So I look along the wrack line." She pointed to the streaks of sea grasses, pebbles, and other debris that were washing onto shore.

"We're looking closely at flotsam and jetsam, right?"

"Yes."

"I've never had a chance to use those words in a sentence before."

Sinclair smiled, which made her happy. She wanted to win her over. This acquisition would be hard won, but no one in New York had ever seen such unique work, and Brenna's gallery had to present it.

"I look for unusual pieces in the rather constant arrangement of pebbles. What I mean is, rocks have a particular overall look and the sea glass will stand out from them."

"It's that easy?"

"Sometimes. Sometimes not. Reading the beach is important. There are places where no glass washes up and others where currents seem to push them. I don't know why, but I've come to find that it's true."

Brenna mimicked Sinclair by talking while keeping her head down, sweeping a concentrated gaze back and forth just ahead of her feet.

"How big are the pieces we're looking for?"

"All different sizes. The bigger the better, but any size is a great find."

"It's like treasure hunting."

"Exactly."

"And easier than diving for sunken pirates' booty."

She looked up and Sinclair smiled again, then bent over and picked something up from the sand and placed it in Brenna's hand. The quarter-sized brown piece felt smooth around the edges. It looked polished and she could see light through it.

"Wow. What do you think this was from?"

"Most likely an old beer bottle."

"From an old beer bottle to this." Brenna rubbed her finger over the sand-worn edges, smoothed by its plunge into the sea.

She began to hand it back and Sinclair said, "Keep it." She put it in her pocket and they continued walking.

After a short while, Brenna spotted something shimmering weakly among some pebbles.

"Is this one?" She held it up for Sinclair.

"Yes. That's a nice one. That color is called ice blue or soft blue. It comes from medicine bottles, ink bottles, and fruit jars. It's probably around a hundred years old."

The glass was pitted with pin-sized holes and Brenna asked her about them.

"Sea glass hydrates, which is the frosty surface you see. Constant contact with water makes the lime and soda in the glass leach out. They combine with other elements and form tiny crystals on its surface."

"And that's what made me find it? It sparkled a little?"

"Exactly." Sinclair grinned again.

A little wave of excitement rippled through Brenna's stomach. She suddenly felt like a student energized by her teacher's approval and giddy from the attention.

❖

They'd been out for about an hour, and Sinclair really enjoyed her time with Brenna. She always hunted alone so her enjoyment surprised her. She'd always imagined another person would hinder her, but having the company of a beautiful, charming woman like Brenna roused her spirits. Today seemed quite different from the often-difficult days of her solitary existence.

Brenna wandered away to search around an abandoned lobster pot that had washed in with the tide, enabling Sinclair to watch her without being obvious. She was probably a couple of inches taller than she was, maybe five foot eight. She had neatly tucked her white button-down shirt into nicely fitting jeans with an expensive-looking designer belt. If things were different, Brenna would be exactly the type of woman Sinclair was attracted to. Her slightly stocky build, brunette hair, and chestnut eyes brought to life the daydreams

Sinclair sometimes allowed herself. And when Brenna rolled up the sleeves of her button-down shirt, revealing the tattooed sleeve on her right arm, electrifying chills ripped through Sinclair. Brenna appeared to be a successful businesswoman with a rebellious streak. Without a doubt, she seemed self-assured, smart, and poised. Also very sexy.

But Sinclair knew such flights of fancy would leave her disappointed and empty in the end. She'd let herself get carried away before and even gone on some dates, but nothing proved to be as fine as the fantasy. And those women had lived locally so it had been easy to pursue her interests. Brenna represented someone she couldn't have and, more important, someone she shouldn't have. Even though what Brenna told her checked out online as legitimate, she couldn't trust just that source.

But as she watched Brenna, engrossed in her search and unbelievably provocative, the rush she allowed herself felt too damn good.

Brenna suddenly yelled, "Look at this!"

Sinclair hurried over to her to see what she'd found. Brenna held up a large piece of ruby-red glass and Sinclair caught her breath.

"Holy moly," she said when Brenna handed her the piece.

"That's a good holy moly, right?"

"Oh, yes. Red is extremely rare, Brenna. And this one looks very old." She looked up at her. "I think you might have part of an automobile taillight here."

"But taillights are plastic."

"Not the ones made before World War II."

They stood close while examining the red glass and Sinclair could feel Brenna's excitement. She loved the way her mouth fell open in astonishment, and a rush of pleasure ran through her.

"Are you kidding? It's been rolling around out there for that long?"

She nodded. "That's why some sea glass is extraordinarily uncommon and very expensive. There's something magical about discovering a piece nestled among the rocks or digging one up in the sand as if the sea partially hid it just for you to find."

Brenna's eyes opened as wide as a child's at Christmas.

"You let me keep the first piece you found this morning, Sinclair. I want you to have this."

"No, this is special. And it's yours." She reached out and tried to give it back, but Brenna wrapped her hands around Sinclair's.

"I have a better idea. I'd like to commission you to make a window with that."

A million thoughts raced through her head, but ideas about designing a window weren't among them. Brenna's touch sizzled. Just her hands, soft and smooth and strong, enfolded hers and made her want to melt into the sand. Sinclair closed her eyes to capture the full feeling and record it forever, but Brenna interrupted her.

"Would you do it?"

"Sure. Sure." But she'd gone over her limit of what was safe. "Let's head back. I'm sure you need to get on the road and I've got work to do."

In the middle of the vast expanse of the beach and ocean, Sinclair strangely felt claustrophobic. She was too close to feeling more than she should. She had to get Brenna in the car, flee to the confines of her house, and close the door on all her foolish feelings.

She turned toward home and began climbing over the boulders.

Brenna caught up with her. "We still need to go over the exhibition details, and you were going to show me your work."

Brenna was right. As much as she wanted to escape her fascination for the New York art dealer, she couldn't just yet. And she really didn't want to.

CHAPTER SEVEN

S inclair's work area was small but efficient. She had enough room to create two pieces at once, with an assortment of sea glass spread out around the window frames.

Brenna leaned over one of the windows to inspect the large sheet of paper underneath.

"So you create a line drawing first and then build the glass pieces to that design?"

"Basically. I need to alter the design as I go since the glass pieces are never the exact shape or size that fits."

She picked up the soldering iron. "And you solder them together?"

Sinclair nodded.

"Kind of like Rosie the Riveter?"

Sinclair laughed. "Without the head kerchief."

"Where do you get the frames?"

Sinclair ran her fingers over one of the window frames. "From remodeled homes and such. Everyone seems to want aluminum windows nowadays so they rip these out and throw them away or leave them on the side of the road for the garbage truck. I have a shed full of them. I love the different patinas on each. Some have faded paint or worm holes. Each one has such personality. I like giving them a new lease on life here."

One window appeared much further along in execution than the other. It consisted of mostly light-green and yellow glass. Brenna pointed to the yellow pieces. "What were these before?"

"They could have come from old Vaseline containers from the 1930s. The bigger green chunks are bottle lips, which give the window a little dimensionality."

"What's the plan for this other window?"

Sinclair reached past her to pick up a shoebox that sat on the far corner of the table, and her arm brushed against Brenna. Immediately, Brenna moved out of the way. Damn, she thought, instantly regretting the message the action probably sent to Sinclair. She certainly didn't want her to think she didn't want to be near her. But she also didn't want to scare her away. They were making good progress in establishing some trust. And while she wasn't used to working on that specific issue with other artists, she had to understand and work with Sinclair's particular needs before doing business with her.

Both Sinclair and Brenna made the polite mumblings of two people trying to excuse any awkwardness caused by their tight proximity. Sinclair moved back and set the box down in front of them.

"Pottery shards?" Brenna said.

"Yes. They wash up on the beach, too."

Brenna sifted through the shards with wonder. Some were white with blue markings and others were brown, like pottery. She picked up a piece of cream and pink porcelain and turned it over and over in her hand. "These are fabulous. Some have impressed pottery marks, but I don't know enough about chinaware to identify them."

"Neither do I, but they're beautiful. That window will be filled with these pieces. Since they're not transparent, I'll add regular stained glass and mix them in together."

"What are the most interesting things you've found?"

"Glass beads, a pharmacist's stirrer, pieces of old Dutch pipes, and lots of buttons. Once, tucked way up in the lee of a larger boulder, I found a ceramic doll's boot."

"Amazing."

"They're all so much fun to incorporate into my work."

"Every piece you make truly is original."

"And a gift from the sea."

Brenna looked up from the box. Sinclair stood very close to her, sharing the excitement of discovery. She was intriguing. This enigmatic woman, searching for the riches that the sea offered, then creating truly unique windows, was as rare as the work. And as exquisite.

She was thinking less about business and more about her increasing attraction to Sinclair, which surprised her. Business always came first. If it hadn't, she wouldn't be in the fortunate position she was. A lot of her peers were struggling to keep their doors open while Brenna could take trips, just like this, to engage in new and promising ventures. She had to remind herself that no matter how beautiful and intriguing she found Sinclair, obtaining the art had to be her number-one goal.

"How many pieces do you currently have?" She needed to focus on procuring the exhibition.

"Counting these and the ones I have in the shed, I'd say twenty."

Performing a quick calculation of the number of linear feet in her gallery, Brenna said, "We'd probably need about five more. Do you think you could do that?"

"It depends on when the show is."

"How much time do you need?"

"A month or two."

"That'll work out very well."

"The collection we got this morning will help quite a bit."

"May I go out with you again? I mean, out hunting for glass?" She still had to get something in writing from Sinclair, to seal an exclusive deal, so she needed to spend another day hunting for sea glass with her.

Sinclair smiled. "Sure."

"When are you leaving?"

"Back to New York?" *Obviously, dummy.*

"Yes."

"Depends on the next low tide."

Sinclair now looked more mischievous than amused. "That'd be in about nine hours."

"Then I'll be back in nine hours."

Sinclair watched Brenna drive away and excitement swirled inside her as she anticipated Brenna's return visit. She smiled as she closed the door, but when she turned toward the windows that faced the ocean, its vastness frightened her.

What was she doing? This woman took her way out of her safety zone. She was much more progressive and sharp than women she had dated previously. Not that the local women were dumb; they just didn't care to venture from their small-town world. They didn't ask her many questions and certainly didn't spend time on the Internet, two activities that she engaged in.

But she couldn't deny her magnetic attraction to Brenna, whose outstanding beauty and personality, as well as her charm, dazzled Sinclair.

It had been a long time since she'd experienced emotions like this. She'd felt them for Donna at the beginning of their relationship, but its lifespan, though sweet and tender, was quite short. And if she compared the two with a percentage, the surge she experienced with Donna was about thirty percent of what now rushed through her.

Could she afford to let her attraction develop? She sure wanted to. However, she well understood the complications that arose from such pursuits of the heart. Statements from past encounters still rung in her head. *"You're so closed up." "I don't really know anything about you." "This wall you have up is too high for me."*

Shit, how long had she been in Pemaquid Point? It was going on twenty years and not once had she let her guard down enough to really fall for someone. Not the way she'd always dreamed she could.

She poured all her romance into her artwork and outwardly lived and loved and adored there. She could substitute her desire for physical closeness by busying her hands and mind with artistic creation. It had fulfilled her and given her satisfaction, but not the kind she truly craved.

The times she did date felt more like rehearsals of a play in which she didn't want to star. She would try to reach out and feel something but found herself just going through the motions. No one had come along to compel her to want to knock that wall over.

Until now, that is.

She looked at the two stained-glass windows awaiting her attention. She had to get back to them but now, instead of filling her life, they'd serve to get her through the nine hours until Brenna returned.

❖

"She's amazing." Brenna walked around her room, her cell phone cradled on her shoulder as she reported back to Carl.

"And how's her artwork?"

"That's what I mean."

"No, honey, it's not. You're chirping like a bird that's found a bag of seeds. She's cute, isn't she?"

Brenna looked out the window of her hotel room. New Harbor was such a beautiful place, with big, healthy trees and a cute, white-steepled church just down the street. "She is. I really like her. And, yes, her art is fantastic as well."

"So you're going to do a show for her?"

"Absolutely, which is why I'm calling. Let's look at the calendar and pencil in something about two months from now."

"Sounds good."

"And could you tell Lucy I'll be staying a little longer?"

"An artist reconnoiter, I suppose?"

"You could say that."

"What do *you* say?"

"Some artists need gentle ego handling, but not this one. But something else about her requires a slow approach. She's…" Brenna struggled for the right word, "an enigma."

"A marketing ploy, perhaps?"

"Just the opposite. She's almost a recluse."

"At the very least, is she a sexy recluse?"

She was. And initially, Brenna hadn't prepared herself for that possibility. "She's beautiful," Brenna said. "She hasn't signed a contract yet so that's why I'm going back there tonight."

"Shall I save my imaginatively impudent comments for when you return?"

"Please."

Brenna hung up and decided to investigate the town. She walked toward its center, which was nothing more than a crossroads. A gas station sat across the street from a fishing supply store. Next to that stood a small market, probably the one that had that great coffee. She had to get some before she left.

She circled back toward her motel and crossed the street toward the Seaside Stop. The thought of a drink and an appetizer made her stomach rumble in the affirmative.

She liked the interior right away. She imagined that the locals embraced the place as a refuge after a day of fishing or work. It felt warm and welcoming, with just the right amount of nautical pictures, fishing gear, and ships' equipment to make it seem authentic and definitely not a tourist trap.

She sat at the bar and ordered a rum and coke from the bartender, a tall, pretty woman in Levi's and a T-shirt. Her smile was kind as she served her the drink.

"Would you like something to eat? We've got mussels, crab, calamari—"

"Crab cakes?"

"Yup, with roasted apple mayonnaise."

"I'd love some."

When the bartender returned with the crab cakes, she said, "From out of town?"

"New York. I'm talking with a local artist about her work."

"We've got a lot of artists around here, that's for sure."

"This one's pretty unique."

"That'd be Sinclair Grady."

Brenna laughed. "Small town, huh?"

"That, and she's the most unique. No one else makes those windows that she does." Wiping her hands on a towel, she added, "She's an old friend of mine. I'm Donna."

She reached out and Brenna took her hand. "Brenna Wright."

"She was okay taking an unannounced visitor?"

"How'd you know I was unannounced?"

"I know she has a computer but no e-mail, not even a land line, and she doesn't advertise."

Brenna bit into a crab cake. "This is fabulous."

"Thanks."

"She wasn't exactly happy to see me. I think she thought I was a tax collector or door-to-door salesman or something."

"She doesn't get much company. Doesn't really want it, actually."

"I got that right away. But once we started talking, she was so friendly. We had a great time. And I'm going back to see her tonight."

"Really?"

Brenna thought the response was curious so she jokingly said, "Why, should you warn me about something?"

"She obviously trusts you. And for her, that's a big statement."

Brenna began to ask why, but Donna stepped away to help a customer and the luscious-looking crab cakes demanded her attention.

CHAPTER EIGHT

B renna and Sinclair were back out on the beach at the next low tide. This time, Sinclair had given her a shoulder bag to collect her findings in.

Sinclair showed her more tricks for searching—to pay attention to tenacious knots of seaweed that could grip the sea glass and to look carefully in clumps of oyster shells and driftwood.

Brenna had never gone to these lengths to sign an artist. She was used to an animated first meeting and then eager negotiations. Still, she didn't mind the sea-glass lessons, and spending time with Sinclair certainly wasn't unbearable.

At one point, she touched Brenna's shoulder. "Look."

A porcupine foraged around a mass of seaweed that covered a lobster carcass, picking at the tender bits.

They took the opportunity to remove their satchels and sit side by side on a rock. The slight ocean breeze scared away what heat the sun provided when it poked its head out every so often. A few lobster boats rocked back and forth on the water, their captains tending to their traps, pulling each one up and inspecting the contents.

"So, all your glass comes from this beach?"

"No. I travel up and down the local coast. I don't leave Maine, but I've heard of great spots along the Hudson River, all over Connecticut and Massachusetts. I'd love to go to Hawaii and Spain. Really, you can find sea glass anywhere, but it helps to know where to look in general."

"Like?"

"Places near old shipping routes from the late 1800s or places where people gathered a long time ago, like turn-of-the-century seaside amusement areas. But artifacts can travel far and wide so you have to be diligent and keep your eyes peeled."

She reached into her bag and pulled out a lozenge-size turquoise-blue piece, worn smooth from time.

"These pieces used to be part of something bigger that was thrown out, washed from the shore, or accidentally fell into the ocean. They got broken apart and were forgotten all these years as they tumbled around, abused by relentless waves of water and sand. Then, one day, they make their way back to shore and we find them. They've come out stronger, more valuable, and vastly unique."

"They reinvented themselves."

"Yes. That's the significant part." She held up the sea glass. "Bits once brilliant, now more beautiful than ever."

"Is that what attracts you to them?"

"I suppose. They're little treasures waiting to be discovered. Some people walk right past them, but I've been enamored with them from the first time I came here."

"When was that?"

"About twenty years ago."

"Did you move here with family?"

Sinclair didn't answer right away. She looked out toward the water, as if searching for something, maybe from long ago. "No."

"You were young."

She nodded. "Fifteen."

"Were you alone?"

"Yes. I," she paused and then shrugged, "I ran away."

"Wow." Brenna didn't know what else to say. She couldn't even conceive of being on her own as an adolescent. Her own family had always been a safe haven, allowing her to be young and not care about too much beyond exploring the world through school and playing with friends.

"I had a bad childhood. I was adopted so they weren't my real parents anyway. They raised me, but I never fit in and was never happy."

"What made you run away?"

Sinclair picked at the rock between her legs. "My family wasn't exactly the Brady Bunch. They liked to hit."

"I'm so sorry." Brenna couldn't imagine what horrors she had experienced.

"My stepfather was a dairy farmer in Waterville, New York. My stepbrother was their only child. They tried for three years to have another but couldn't, so my stepmother finally talked her husband into adopting me when I was a baby. He didn't want a girl. He wanted a boy to help my stepbrother and him on the farm." She hesitated as if mulling over what else she should say. Looking up, she said, "I usually don't talk about this."

"You don't have to if it's difficult."

"It was a long time ago and I'm far away from it all." Sinclair shrugged. "I think my stepmother didn't want another boy that would turn out to be abusive like my stepbrother, who was beginning to use his fists on her like her husband was. So they got me."

Sinclair looked back down and resumed the rock-picking. "When I was ten, I came home from school and a sheriff's car and a brown van were at our place. My stepfather was sitting on the porch and told me not to go inside. I asked why and he said my stepmother was dead. Then he told me to clean the water trough. Instead, I stood there and started crying. He backhanded me and I landed on my butt."

"Oh, my God, Sinclair."

"That's what I was raised to know. So when I was old enough, I just ran away. I eventually ended up here, and an elderly woman named Peggy took me in. She had three grandkids of her own, dropped off by her wayward daughter years before. She had no husband but she had a lot of love to give. She found me outside the local market," Sinclair pointed vaguely toward town, "and asked me where my folks were. I told her I'd run away and she took me inside, had me pick out whatever I wanted to eat, and took me home."

"How long did you live with Peggy?"

"Six years. When I was seventeen, I took two jobs and finally saved enough to buy a house when I turned twenty-one. Peggy told me she owned this rental house on the beach. It was in bad shape because it had a leaky roof, no heating, and old electrical wiring, but she offered it to me and carried my loan so I didn't have to qualify. When I started my artwork, I juggled that and my two jobs until I could pay off most of the house. And then she died a few years ago. I was devastated. She really tried to care for me all the way to the end," she said, "because she had willed the house to me."

"That was a very loving and sweet thing to do."

"Her grandkids didn't mind either. They had all moved away by then, and I don't see them much anymore."

"So what keeps you here?"

Sinclair stopped studying her rock and lifted her head. Her expression was hard to read, as if she didn't understand the purpose of the question.

"I mean, do you have lots of friends here, or a love interest?"

She looked back out over the water. The lobster boats were heading south, motoring slowly about a hundred yards off the shore. "The ocean keeps me here."

Brenna wasn't sure if she did have someone special, but if she did, it evidently wasn't any of her business so she didn't pry any further.

"Well, I can tell you one thing," Brenna said as she stretched and felt her lower back ache a little from all the bending over. "I haven't slowed down like this in a while. My cell phone isn't ringing and I don't have any appointments to rush off to. This is great."

"Type-A personalities usually don't do well around these parts."

"You think I'm a type A?"

Sinclair's concentrated stare came with a side of smirk. "Not only present but fueled with lots of caffeine. Plus, you have all the tell-tale symptoms. You just named a few."

Brenna resisted the urge to check her cell phone, like she did often during the day, and smiled. "Okay, you've got me there. But this type-A lady is going to take your artwork to the Big Apple."

"For now, just enjoy the downtime."

"That's certainly easy to do here." Brenna took in the entire coast. "I'm beginning to comprehend why your work has such an emotional effect on me. You're out here, taking pieces of real things, of timeworn treasures, and translating them into art. You feel the history in the sea glass."

"You understand a lot, then."

"Art is the transmission of feeling the artist has experienced."

"That's Tolstoy."

"That's you, too."

"I'd like to think that if I was born into any time period, I'd be plunked down right in the middle of Post-Impressionism. What an exciting time in art history."

"Oh, I agree. Can you imagine sharing a cup of tea with Gauguin or Toulouse-Lautrec and listening to them talk about bending and exaggerating their painting subjects to convey that its emotional effect was central to their work?"

"I'd give my right arm to spend time with any of them."

Brenna smiled. "Imagine being there when they were all fired up about rejecting the limitations of their predecessors. They were true rebels."

"If I could go back and pick one to have dinner with it'd be…" Sinclair stopped to ponder a moment, and just as she turned to Brenna to answer, they said simultaneously, "Van Gogh!"

"What a master," Brenna said. "I was at the Van Gogh Museum—"

"In Amsterdam?"

"Yes. His work overwhelmed me." She held her hand to her chest as if holding in the heart that wanted to ardently spill out from the memory. "I stood in front of *Wheatfield with Crows* for at least thirty minutes, studying the turbulence in his brushstrokes."

"I'd love to see his work up close," Sinclair said. "It's all so intense. I don't think it's necessarily true that he was symbolically expressing loneliness in the barren fields or death in the foreboding look of the crows, but it's hard not to feel those things. I mean, his vivid and jarring execution shows us such extreme passion."

Brenna agreed. "I look at those paintings and always think about the fact that when he couldn't take life anymore he walked out to the same fields where he painted and shot himself there."

They were silent for a moment. Then Brenna asked, "Can art exist without passion?"

"I don't think so. At least I hope not. I mean, think about that time in history. It must have been electrifying to break out of the traditionally objective way of painting what they saw and instead be the first ones to express themselves primarily through their inner experiences. How momentous to have the courage and freedom to distort reality and let their pure emotions out onto canvas."

"Exactly."

A ship's horn blared in the distance and they stopped talking for a while. The nippy sea air picked up, chilling Brenna's cheeks. Her thoughts seemed to be as clear as they'd ever been. She was enjoying her spontaneous vacation. Carl could easily handle the exhibition setup and would call her if he had any problems. She had nothing else pressing at the moment, and that realization allowed her to inhale the salty, invigorating air deeply.

"Brenna, I haven't…" Sinclair said after a while, but faltered. "No one really knows about my childhood. I'm surprised with myself for telling you. My past is pretty much a closed door."

Brenna listened and nodded gently.

"I keep to myself quite a bit and don't make friends easily. Part of me was furious with myself for talking to you about it at all."

When Sinclair looked at her with vulnerable, inquiring eyes, Brenna said, "I understand. I respect your feelings, so please don't regret talking to me."

"I mean, we just met," Sinclair said. "I'm afraid you'll think differently of me."

"I don't at all."

Sinclair studied her as if searching for sincerity. An unanticipated urge to hug her washed over Brenna, but instead she pushed her knee into Sinclair's. "Really."

Though her smile looked a little strained, Sinclair seemed relieved and said, "Would you like to continue this discussion over some dinner?"

"I'd love to."

❖

Sinclair made a light dinner of salad with pasta al pesto, opened a bottle of wine, and arranged a picnic blanket on the floor, close to her diminutive fireplace. They sat side by side, facing the flames. Two oak logs crackled inside the brick-lined opening, offering a welcome invitation to warm up from the dampness quickly settling over Pemaquid Point.

Their segue from talking about Post-Impressionism out on the rocks to the current topic of the Rococo period would have seemed a fairly natural transition, but the dialogue in between had followed an odd path that included instructions for making authentic Maine lobster rolls and a short dialogue on the advantages of having 24-hour pharmacies, 24-hour computer stores, and even 24-hour facials in Manhattan.

"Rococo was a waste of oil paint and marble." Sinclair sipped her wine and looked mischievously at Brenna.

"But coming out of the Baroque period, where everything felt heavy and sometimes harsh, don't you think the world deserved a little fantasy and lightheartedness?"

"I'm suspect of any art that the Roman Catholic Church encouraged, especially an art form used to impress people by expressing victorious power and control."

Brenna laughed, knowing that Sinclair's sideways grin meant she was mostly debating for the fun of the argument. She did have some very good points, but the stance was meant to be playful. "So, Bernini's *Ecstasy of St. Theresa* is a piece of crap?"

"Oh, I wouldn't go that far. She's beautiful."

"But she's actually a prime example of true Baroque art."

"I stand corrected. But she's the prime example of a gorgeous woman, no matter what century. I'm referring to the feathery mess that made up most paintings and ornamentation."

"Rococo was beautiful in its lavishness, don't you think?"

"Not to the tune of fluffy ruffles and ethereal refinement. I don't find morality in it anywhere. It existed for the aristocracy, not common folk."

"You're just being stuffy. Like a noble Rococo lady."

"Bite your tongue."

"You're wearing me out." Brenna leaned back on her hands, moving her feet closer to the fire. "Were you the captain of the debate team in high school?"

"I never went to high school."

"Really?"

She shook her head. "I was afraid to. I was new here and without my stepparents. Peggy didn't make me."

"So how did you learn so much about the arts?"

"The public library. While her grandkids were in school, I'd hide in the library and read. It was my very own safe world."

Brenna couldn't imagine what Sinclair must have gone through. Her childhood was virtually the opposite of hers. While she had safety and normalcy, Sinclair must have had uncertainty and irregularity. "It must have been hard."

"It was at first. But anything was better than being in my stepparents' house."

"Were they verbally abusive as well as physically?"

"I don't really want to talk about that."

"I'm sorry." Brenna winced inside. "I had no right to ask."

"It was a long time ago."

Sinclair shrugged, but Brenna could tell by the sadness pulling on her face that the horror she must have experienced could never truly be trivialized. "I've never been accused of being tactful."

"It's okay. I just don't talk about it much. But I would like to know something about you."

"Sure."

"Tell me about your tattoo."

Brenna raised her arm and pulled up her sleeve, and Sinclair moved closer to inspect the ink that began at her wrist and ended at her shoulder. She touched Brenna's arm and said, "It's a mermaid."

"I had a whole underworld seascape done." She showed her how the mermaid wrapped around her forearm and intertwined with a beautiful octopus, a seahorse, and a starfish. The background was a complement of varying blues and purples, which highlighted the oranges and reds and yellows of the sea life.

"The small bubbles give the whole tattoo dimension. It's like an exquisite painting."

"Thanks. I really love it. It took about a year from start to finish."

"Really? Did it hurt?"

"Yes."

Sinclair laughed. "You don't mince words, do you?"

"No."

Sinclair ran her finger gently up and down her arm, following the artwork, as if she were drawing it herself. Brenna almost closed her eyes with the pleasure of her soothing touch but thought doing that might make her seem too desirous. Still, her mesmerizing strokes made it hard to think or speak.

"I really like how the colors blend on the mermaid's tail."

"Uh-huh." Brenna swallowed.

"The needles must be really small to get this detail…" Sinclair looked up and must have understood the look on Brenna's face because her one-finger stroking changed to four fingers that slowly caressed up and down her arm.

"I'm hypnotizing you, aren't I?" Her roguish smile had powerful appeal.

"Uh-huh."

"So, how about thirty percent for your exhibition fee?"

"Okay."

Sinclair stopped caressing and wrapped her warm hand around Brenna's forearm. With a squeeze she said, "I'm just kidding. I wouldn't take advantage of you when you're compromised."

Brenna blinked away the yearning for more strokes and smiled unhurriedly. "Good thing. I think you found my weak spot."

"Should I continue and then ask for your car keys as well?"

"And the keys to my flat in the city while you're at it."

Brenna laughed but noticed Sinclair's expression had frozen in what looked like sudden hesitation.

"I'm sorry," Brenna said. "That was probably too forward. I was truly just kidding."

Sinclair seemed to catch herself, blinking away her uncertainty. "I guess I knocked the type A right out of you for a second."

Brenna didn't know where Sinclair had gone just then, but she seemed to be back. "Today has been one of the best days I can remember. When taxi horns are blaring and helicopters are flying overhead in the city, it's hard to empty your brain and relax." She picked up her glass of wine and took a sip. "But I've gotten to relax all day."

"I'm glad."

CHAPTER NINE

What foreign person has taken over my body? Here she was, sitting in front of her fireplace with a woman she'd met only a couple of days before, and she was rattlebrained and wound up. She couldn't believe how straightforwardly she had reached out to touch Brenna's arm. Sure, wanting to inspect the tattoo had been a good reason, but she probably would have asked to count her freckles as long as she could feel that smooth skin. And the powerful desire to have physical contact with Brenna came from a long-ago place she considered unreachable or, at the very least, unresponsive due to the slow death of her neglected heart.

Sinclair hadn't been this excited to be around someone in a long time. Actually, maybe ever. She pursued her desire for women on occasion, but the effort sometimes came more from the need to fend off her long bouts of cabin fever or to warm prolonged winter nights than from a true desire for a particular person.

But if being bowled over by someone feels this fantastic, then keep the strikes coming.

Type-A Brenna from New York seemed really easy-going once she slowed down and tuned in to sea-glass hunting. Her animated interest seemed to mean she was truly thrilled to find the sea's treasures. Her intelligence and humor captivated Sinclair, too. She hadn't talked to someone nonstop in years, if ever. She'd never really let someone in like that.

The familiar clutch of distrust, that would constantly originate in her stomach and flood her body, didn't come. For some reason she could relax into Brenna and throw her worries right out into the surf.

Although alarm bells should start clanging in her head, for once the urge to put her guard up had disappeared. She allowed herself to feel comfortable and secure, though it could prove to be a dangerous mistake. But just for tonight, she told herself, it would be okay.

Brenna put her wineglass back down on the floor by the fire. "I must admit, I was a bit intimidated when you first walked up to me on the beach."

Sinclair looked down a moment and then back up. "Oh, that. I'm sorry. I'm a pretty private person and I don't like surprises."

"Well, I came unannounced so it's really my fault. But I'm glad I did. A letter just wouldn't have been as enjoyable."

"And you wouldn't have gotten dinner out of it."

"I loved it." Brenna patted her stomach, then glanced at her watch. "My lord, it's late. I should get out of your hair. I'm sure low tide is early tomorrow."

Sinclair pointed to the tide clock on her wall. "It'll be at 6:40 a.m. so I can sleep in."

Brenna looked at her, eyes narrowing slightly. "We city folk stay up into the wee hours. I shouldn't corrupt you with my wicked habits. Plus, I need to get back to the Pine Cottages soon."

"The oldest hotel in Maine."

"Is it really?"

Sinclair chuckled. "No, but the locals say it is. The structure leans toward the north a bit, but it hasn't fallen down, so I think you're safe."

"That's a good thing because all my paperwork is in the room. I have to go over some homework and check in at the gallery."

Sinclair stood and Brenna followed her to the kitchen with the dishes.

"The gallery's still open?"

"Until eleven. But the staff is staying later than that right now to get a show ready for opening."

Sinclair walked Brenna to her door. When she opened it and Brenna stepped out onto the stoop, Sinclair said, "I think we're forgetting something."

Brenna hesitated, then nodded her understanding almost timidly. She leaned forward and gently kissed Sinclair. Their lips lingered together for a few seconds, and Sinclair thought the dizziness that suddenly came over her would cause her legs to collapse.

When she pulled away, all she could see were Brenna's blissful chestnut-brown eyes.

Sinclair's heart beat in her ears and she sank into the door frame for support. "That wasn't what I meant when I said we were forgetting something, but that...that was wonderful."

Brenna's eyes opened wider. "Oh. What did we forget?"

"The details of the exhibition."

Brenna touched a finger to her chin. "I'm so sorry, I—"

"Don't be. That was better than what I was thinking." She placed her hand on the side of Brenna's waist. "I'd love to see you tomorrow if you can. Maybe nine or ten?"

"I promise to talk about the exhibition this time."

"I'll hold you to that."

Sinclair watched Brenna walk to her car and get in. Through her windshield Brenna waved and Sinclair held up her hand.

Sleep wouldn't come very easily tonight. She had been keyed up all day, but that kiss had sent her heart into hyperspace.

Chapter Ten

S inclair had been back from her beachcombing for a couple of hours and anxiously awaited Brenna's arrival. The sun had warmed her as she collected some unusually large and perfect pieces of sea glass and skipped up the stairs to her house. She felt alive and laughed at her own silliness. She lightheartedly glided around the front room, straightening up and vacuuming the rugs. Even Petey the squirrel seemed happy for her because he was rolling around on the warm wooden deck.

She was eager to finish the windows she and Brenna had discussed that would round out the collection for the exhibition in New York.

When she heard a car approach, she cheerfully opened the door. Brenna pulled up and got out, beaming. It looked as though she'd also benefited from a great morning.

"Hi, there," Brenna said as she reached Sinclair at the door.

"Hi, yourself."

This time, Sinclair leaned forward to kiss Brenna, the contact as tender and gentle as the night before. She really liked Brenna and thought it might be mutual. Their attraction could heat up and move toward something a lot more intense, and maybe that wasn't a smart thing to do, but for now this felt right.

They spent the morning touring Sinclair's shed and Brenna praised every window she showed, which delighted Sinclair.

When they returned to the house just past noon, Sinclair fixed lunch and they sat next to each other at the table, devouring big bowls of chowder and toast in no time.

"I'll have a contract drafted and sent to you," Brenna said as she dabbed her mouth with a napkin. "Just let me know if you have any questions. It's a standard boilerplate contract, and fairly simple."

Sinclair stacked her toast dish on top of her empty bowl. "What happens if the windows sell?"

"You mean *when* they sell. We handle all the details, take our percentage, and send you the check. Whatever you don't sell, which should be very few, if any at all, we ship back. We'll need your estimation of the value of each piece because we also cover them on an insurance rider for you. You and I should discuss each one's value since I think you need to charge more than you do now."

"You really think so?"

"Absolutely. It's time to raise your artistic worth. I've been selling art a long time and know where the market is from year to year. We price them reasonably so we create a buzz and then, for future work, the prices can increase from there."

"Supply and demand, huh?"

"It certainly works that way. It'll be up to you to determine how frequently you construct each new piece. Some artists create very few new things and, depending on their popularity, the fewer pieces go for a lot more because of their scarcity. You don't have to work that way, though. I don't really like to control the market deliberately, but the timing has to work for the artist."

"That makes sense." Sinclair got up from the table and took their dishes to the sink.

"Good. I'll arrange to have your windows shipped to the gallery. We'll have them hung about three days before opening night, so plan on getting there around the same time. You'll be able to change anything you'd like."

Startled, Sinclair said, "I'm not going to New York."

Brenna stared at her for the briefest of moments before saying, "What?"

"I'm not going to New York."

"No, I heard that. But what do you mean? Opening night is designed specifically for the art buyers to meet the artist. The bulk of the sales occurs then. There's nothing like meeting the artist of the piece you're buying. It adds a special importance to the provenance of the work."

"I appreciate that, but I'm not going."

"But, Sinclair, it's a huge night." She shook her head and lifted her opened hands, palms up. "That one evening makes the difference between being unknown and exploding onto the art scene."

"No."

"Why not?"

Sinclair looked down, not wanting to meet the increasingly stressful look on Brenna's face. "I'm not interested in becoming known."

"Do you want to sell your art?"

"Of course. But I won't go."

"You're being unreasonable, Sinclair. You have to attend the opening!"

Brenna's voice rose and Sinclair looked up, frustrated. "Are you always this pushy?"

"Pushy? I'm trying to help you!"

She pointed to the floor. "This, right here, isn't helping."

Brenna threw her hands into the air and they came back down with a slap on the sides of her thighs. "This is how it works, Sinclair. I take care of the art and you take care of showing up."

It was her turn to raise her voice. "I'm not leaving Pemaquid Point."

"Why?"

"I don't want to talk about it."

"Well, if we're going to do this show, I need to know why."

"Actually, you don't." She knew she was being difficult but she just couldn't tell her more.

"Sinclair, please consider that this is really important. We can work out whatever you have against going to New York."

"No, we can't."

"It's not like I'm asking you to move there. It's just for a few days."

Panic rose inside Sinclair. She was caught between wanting something so much but knowing she couldn't allow it. "I said no."

"So now you're going to back out?"

"If that's what it means."

"I don't know what any of this means!" Brenna had become extremely agitated, her hands punctuating every word.

Sinclair knew she was being unpleasantly mulish but anger bubbled over as well. "It means I'm not going to New York."

"Sinclair—"

"I'm not talking about this any more!"

Brenna shook her head in small movements as if her frustration was causing tremors. Her face grew red. "You think I'm pushy? Well, you're being pretty damn obstinate, so I guess we're stymied."

"I guess so."

Brenna opened her mouth to say something, then closed it. She stood, fished car keys out of her pocket, then shook her head again, but this time, Sinclair knew she'd thoroughly thwarted Brenna.

She turned and walked out the door.

Sinclair listened for the car to start, and when the gravel crackling under the tires receded, giving way to a desolate silence even the waves couldn't drown out, she felt more alone than ever.

❖

"Damn it to hell." Brenna stomped around the gallery. Her fourth cup of coffee sloshed around in its mug. "This is fucking ridiculous." She'd driven all that way to hand Sinclair a golden goose, and Sinclair had thrown it back in her face.

"I know you're not agoraphobic," she said aloud, "because you said you traveled up and down the coast looking for sea glass. So what's up your ass about New York?"

She ran through a hundred scenarios. Was Sinclair worried about the crime in the city? Had something bad happened to her there? Was she afraid to tell her she couldn't afford the trip? Did she think she wouldn't fit in with the Manhattan crowd?

And why had Sinclair become so angry? It was as if she was being asked to commit a crime or step off a dangerous, rocky ledge.

Had she been too pushy, like Sinclair had said? She looked out the window for a moment before saying to herself, Oh, hell, no. I'm doing my business and arranging for an exhibition that any artist in the world would give their last meal to have.

But Sinclair has demands.

What the fuck?

Brenna swiped at the counter and tapped a furious staccato that did nothing but irritate her more. She stopped and took stock of her thoughts.

In the past, she'd handled much more volatile situations with more control and composure than she'd exhibited at Sinclair's. So, what made her fly off the handle like that?

It was the kiss. Well, more than the kiss. She'd really started to like Sinclair, and her enthusiasm had moved far beyond the excitement of the exhibition. Everything had been going so well. She was feeling so much for this creative, beautiful artist. She'd relaxed around her and everything seemed to click perfectly. And when Sinclair put her foot down, Brenna realized that not only her business deal was getting stomped on, but her personal feelings as well.

Rejection had come on two levels, an experience frustrating and new to Brenna.

And strangely, even when they argued, she was so damn attracted to her. Sinclair was feisty and aggressive. She stood her ground in her decisions as doggedly as Brenna had.

They'd both gone from zero to sixty in seconds, and though artists did that all the time, Brenna could control the urge. She was mad at herself for losing her cool. Such a flare-up hadn't allowed for them to strike a constructive compromise. What surprised her the most, though, wasn't the sudden clash between them, but the fact that it had kind of turned her on.

Still, the compulsion to charge out of Sinclair's house and drive away was so strong and familiar that she acted on it without question. She couldn't think of any other way to react.

How dare Sinclair cop such an arrogant attitude? She had no idea what Brenna was offering her. But then again, Brenna needed that art maybe more than Sinclair needed to show it. It would be such a coup to bring it to New York.

She looked around the gallery. It was essential to make another indelible impression with the art press. There was too much competition in the city and Brenna had a sure thing. Well, she almost had it.

She had to go back and convince Sinclair to show her work. Her business was too important not to. She could certainly handle her growing feelings for the artist and secure the artwork.

CHAPTER ELEVEN

Sinclair hated how their evening had ended two days before. She felt silly that she hadn't figured out that an exhibition of her work would require her to attend. Typically, she delivered her pieces to Kay at the Breakers Gallery and never saw who bought them.

The assumption that she'd travel to New York had stunned her, and her reaction was pathetically rude. No wonder Brenna had just up and left. She hadn't given her much choice.

But she didn't want their last time together to end like that. Brenna had obviously left believing her to be a discourteous, unpleasant artist.

The dishes from her breakfast were finally done. She hadn't had the energy to accomplish much since the confrontation with Brenna. Flipping the dish towel over her shoulder, she propped herself against the counter with a thud.

Everything had happened so quickly. She rolled the events backward in her mind, and a clear picture of her first glimpse of Brenna standing on the beach came into view. Her insides had constricted with surprise and caution. She'd thought, who's this person and why is she invading my territory?

The same hackles of irritation and defense prickled up her neck again. She had the right to be suspicious; people didn't just show up unannounced.

And then, she'd let her guard down, inviting this woman into her world, and she turned out to be delightful and funny. But she'd also been pushy about New York and Sinclair had gone into fight mode.

Brenna hadn't deserved such uncivil treatment. Instead of being such an ass, Sinclair could have simply and politely refused.

A knock on the door startled her out of her ruminations.

Cracking the door open, she was even more shocked to see who it was.

"May I come in?" Brenna said.

She opened the door wider, stepped aside, and heard a soft "thank you" as Brenna walked past her.

"Listen," Sinclair said right away. "I'm sure you're used to muggers and purse snatchers in New York, but all we have here are idiots."

Brenna shook her head. "You're not an idiot."

"I'm sorry," they said at once.

"No, I'm the one that needs to apologize." Sinclair held up her hand. "You were just arranging for the exhibition, an offer I'm lucky to get. And I'm the one who smacked you over the head with a mallet."

Brenna took the hand she held up and grasped it tight. "I didn't listen to you. I'm not good at being told no and it showed. All I did was confront you without listening better to what you were trying to say."

"I don't go very far from my home. I know that sounds stupid, but I've been ensconced in Maine for twenty years and feel safe here."

Brenna nodded. "Listen, I'm really sorry, Sinclair. Obviously you have a good reason for not wanting to go."

Sinclair still didn't feel comfortable enough to try to say anything.

Brenna took her other hand. "What is it? Can you tell me, please?"

"I'm not good with big cities."

"Okay. I can understand that. I mean, New York can be a scary place." Her voice grew softer. "But it's also my home, like Pemaquid Point is for you. I grew up in the city and know every inch of Manhattan." Brenna squeezed her hands. "I've got an idea. Would you come with me to New York long before the opening, just for a day or two? You'll be with me the entire time. I'll never let you out of my sight. I'll show you it's not as bad as you may think. And if you don't like it, you can go right home."

The not-being-good-with-big-cities part wasn't really a lie. It was more like a general statement that was much easier to confess than the real reason.

She hadn't left coastal Maine for years, but the desire to travel often pulled at her. She had almost ventured out a few times in the past, but resisted. The risk was too high. She kept her life so carefully guarded and didn't want to ruin the safe zone she'd worked two decades to establish.

However, this was an amazing opportunity for her artwork to be shown in the largest city in America, to really make something of all the hours she toiled at it. But the obvious perils made her hesitate. The exposure could be perilous for her personally.

And yet, Brenna's arrival made a huge difference. She hadn't planned it nor had she ever even dreamt of meeting someone who affected her in such a romantic way. Going to New York with Brenna would allow them to spend more time together, and the notion excited her.

Conversely, rebuffing Brenna ensured her safety and life would return to normal. But was normal good enough now, especially when she had an opportunity to take a chance, both in her career and her love life? If she'd never met Brenna, contemplating the possibilities would be moot. But now that she *had* come into her life, watching her walk away would break her spirit from that day on. Remaining the old maid of coastal Maine made her shiver.

"Sinclair, will you try that?"

Brenna had returned after she had virtually kicked her out the door. Her hands were as warm as sunshine and as powerful as the sea. The woman who stood before her was more than compelling, and

Sinclair's chest ached with want. She was exceedingly attracted to Brenna, who was so gently persuasive and had even guaranteed her wellbeing. The prospect of visiting her seemed scary but reasonable.

She looked into Brenna's eyes. This is going against everything I trust. Please mean what you say, she thought. Show me it's not as bad as I fear. "Okay. A quick trip, that's all."

Brenna pulled her close and kissed her tenderly. "It'll be wonderful."

CHAPTER TWELVE

B renna hurried around the gallery, as she had for the last three days, nervous about Sinclair's imminent arrival. She should be more anxious about the upcoming exhibition, but From the Hand of the Artist would open with huge success. People were already inquiring about purchasing pieces, but no red dots would be placed on any artwork until opening night. Things were moving smoothly. Along with Carl and his first-rate staff keeping all the details well under control, Lucy was coordinating the catering and AV system as well as managing the gallery's daily business.

But even if the show was in trouble, she wouldn't be as tense as she was right now.

She needed that exhibition. Her gut screamed that it would be a huge success. She promised Sinclair that she'd be glad she came to New York. In some ways, it seemed like a tall order because Brenna couldn't control an entire city. But she reviewed her carefully planned itinerary more than twice and everything looked good.

For God's sake, what could go wrong? Get her here, show her around, and sign the contract.

A glance at her watch indicated that Sinclair would arrive any minute. The sun was low, not far from setting, and she hoped Sinclair could find her way here through the busy streets. All she could do now was trust that the next couple of days would go well.

She walked toward the back room, then turned toward the front door.

"Relax," Carl said as he breezed by her. "You're acting like Sinclair Grady is the Queen of England."

"Oh, she's much younger and doesn't wear hats."

"That's more like it. Loosen up, have fun, and remember to use your dental dam."

"Geez, Carl."

Most of his staffers shook their heads in disgust, but Carl just lifted his scissor-wielding hand and punctuated the air. "Shazam."

Brenna walked over to Lucy's desk and leaned against it.

"You want me to book a restaurant for you two tonight?"

"Thanks, but no. I'm taking her to my parents'."

"To the Wrights'? Good, home cooking. That'll be nice."

"I hope. And I'll be off work tomorrow. We're going to stay low-key and—"

Lucy nodded toward the front door. Brenna turned around to see Sinclair walk in. She wore tight jeans and a white-and-yellow peasant top. Her hair glowed from the sun behind her, and Brenna's heart leapt as if she were witnessing an aura from heaven.

Seeing her in the doorway sent ripples of excitement through her. The notion of an exhibition and legal contracts evaporated as quickly as steam off a coffee mug. She looked...stunning. Brenna hurried to greet her and pulled her into a hug. "I'm so glad you're here! I haven't been able to do anything productive all day because I've been waiting to see you."

"It's good to see you, too. That was a long drive."

"Did you park in my spot on the side of the building? Was it easy to find?"

"Yes, everything went well."

Carl glided up behind them. "You're gorgeous."

"Sinclair, this is Carl, my assistant curator."

Sinclair offered her hand. "It's very nice to meet you."

"And it's fascinating to meet someone who can turn Brenna into a hairball."

Brenna put her arm around Sinclair and guided her toward Lucy. "I'm a little nervous."

"So am I."

"Lucy, please meet Sinclair. This is Lucy, my assistant."

Lucy stood and shook her hand. "Welcome to New York."

"Thank you." She looked around at the paintings and photographs. "I love your gallery."

"I want to take you on a tour, but first, I'd like to get you fed. Are you hungry?"

"Very much so."

"Your car will be safe parked behind the gallery. We'll take mine. I hope it's okay that we eat at my parents' place. They're excited to meet you, and my mom cooks a lot better than I do."

Brenna relaxed when Sinclair said, "That'd be nice."

❖

"They're here!"

Sinclair heard what must have been Brenna's mother's voice as Brenna unlocked the door to their brownstone. A woman the height of Brenna, with the same brunette hair and chestnut eyes, hurried in with a wide smile.

"You must be Sinclair. I'm Sandy."

Brenna's mom hugged her tight and Sinclair involuntarily stiffened. She wasn't used to this family gesture and hoped no one would notice her reaction.

"It's very nice to meet you."

Before wrapping Brenna in her arms, Sandy called out, "Mack, the girls are here. Beanie?"

Brenna introduced her father and sister, their arms also open wide. More bear hugs ensued but Sinclair managed to get through it all.

"I'll give you the short tour." Brenna took her hand while Sandy, Mack, and Beanie went to the kitchen.

Sinclair took in the hardwood floors and high ceilings of the living room. One wall had exposed brick, which she loved right away. It gave a nice textured backdrop to the teak furniture and contemporary fixtures.

"This is a pre-war brownstone that my parents bought right after I graduated from college. Beanie and I grew up in Yonkers, but my parents always wanted to live in the Upper West Side, so when I was on my own, they could afford a two-bedroom place."

They peeked in each bedroom and Sinclair liked the tranquil feel of their home. It was worlds apart from where she grew up. No fist-sized holes in the wall or unmatched and broken furniture.

"Are you okay?" Brenna looked concerned.

"I'm just a little nervous."

"Okay." Brenna smiled. "I'm right here. Anything you need, just tell me. If you want to leave, no matter when it is, we'll go."

They walked through the dining alcove that had a beautiful teak table and matching china cabinet filled with what looked like very elegant china. They joined Brenna's family in the kitchen, which had dark-green granite counters, cherry cabinets, polished chrome appliances, and a warm, amber glow from recessed ceiling lights.

"We've got wine, soda, and lots of juice, Sinclair. And Mack makes a mean mai tai. What would you like?"

"Wine would be fine, thanks."

Sandy hugged Brenna again. "I missed you, honey." She smiled at Sinclair and said, "It's been a while since you brought someone over, Brenna."

"It has." Brenna's answer seemed a bit clipped.

"Are you okay, honey?" Sandy's voice remained chipper but her words puzzled Sinclair.

"Mom, I'm fine." Brenna looked at her. "I'm better than fine."

"I got into NYU!" Beanie said.

"That's great!' Brenna high-fived her sister and said to Sinclair, "She's getting her Masters degree in international education, and NYU has a very good program."

Mack put his arm around Beanie. "She'll be close to home and she doesn't even mind living with us for the next four years."

"Congratulations," Sinclair said. She didn't want to compare the Wrights to Ozzie and Harriet, but she had no other applicable reference.

Dinner was unbelievable. Sandy made grilled flatbreads with caramelized onions, sausage, and manchego cheese before serving a grilled leg of lamb in what must have been red wine with mustard and sage. They also had grilled sweet peppers and corn followed by a scrumptious nectarine-blackberry crisp.

Throughout dinner, they all caught each other up on news and events, including Sinclair in everything, explaining backstories and family history.

Halfway through dinner though, Sinclair grew uncertain and scared. She was so far from home and more vulnerable than she'd ever been. She looked around the room, searching for a way to escape, but a squeeze from Brenna's hand interrupted her. Brenna's furrowed brow was asking if something was wrong, and Sinclair shook her head in response. Obviously Brenna knew something was up, but Sinclair couldn't talk about how small and frightened she felt.

She took a deep breath and tuned back in to the conversation at the table. The Wrights were a close clan and really seemed to love each other. Peggy and her grandkids had been somewhat like the Wrights, but Sinclair had never felt a part of them. And witnessing the interaction between Brenna and her kin made her heart ache and yearn at the same time. They were an intact family who supported one another and cared for each other's well-being. Sadness spread throughout her chest. She'd never imagined that such a loving family could ever really exist.

"What about you?" Sandy asked Sinclair when they started on dessert.

"Me? Well, I live in Maine, on the coast."

"It's a beautiful place, Mom," Brenna said. "She's right on the ocean."

Sandy nodded slowly, as if placing more emphasis on her next words. "That's quite a ways away. Is your family close by?"

"Peggy, the woman who raised me, has passed away, but I live in one of her houses now." How much were they going to ask about her background?

"So, your parents aren't around?"

She glanced at Brenna, who was watching her with compassion.

"No. I was on my own when I was fifteen. But I had someone who took care of me. And she encouraged my artwork and helped my career. That's how I met Brenna." Maybe fast-forwarding to her adult life would fend off questions about her childhood.

"So you two met recently?" Sandy seemed to be probing a bit, and Sinclair's stomach tightened.

Brenna must have understood her feelings because she quickly said, "We're going to exhibit her artwork. She makes amazing stained-glass windows from sea glass, but I already told you that."

"You did," Mack said, and turned to Sinclair. "She's been talking nonstop about you."

Brenna smiled and looked down at her food.

"Look at that, Sandy. Brenna got bashful."

Sandy nodded. "Now that's a trait we don't see much." She looked at Brenna as if she was almost happy about it, which confused Sinclair.

Beanie chimed in. "That's not my sister. What did you do with my sister?"

"Stop it, you all. I do have some humility, you know."

"My sister is the strongest, most confident person I know. Whatever she wants, she gets. I don't mean people, Sinclair. I just mean things in life."

"Okay, that's enough about me."

Sinclair liked Brenna's family, and seeing her interact with them made her like Brenna that much more. Still, she fought the anxiety that roiled just below her skin.

Chapter Thirteen

It was close to midnight when they finally left. Mack had brought out a domino game called Mexican Train, which was easy to learn, and they played and laughed until Brenna finally put up her hands and politely dragged Sinclair away.

Brenna served as tour guide, explaining the areas they drove through on their way back to her place. She said she lived in Midtown West and pulled into the underground parking structure of a tall building on 5th Avenue.

She held Sinclair's suitcase and punched the elevator button for the eighteenth floor and soon they were standing at her door.

"How are you feeling?" Brenna's voice was so gentle.

"Tired but good." After a moment, she said, "Is your mother okay with us?"

"Why do you ask?"

"Just a feeling I got."

Brenna kissed her. "My mom is protective of me. Please don't let that influence you."

When they stepped into the entryway inside Brenna's flat, Sinclair took in the entire place. It was very modern, with large picture windows that ran the length of the space. The romantic view of the city and its sparkling lights, framed by sheer drapes, overwhelmed her and filled her with anticipation. The large room that looked like a combination living room, dining room, and entertainment area was spectacular. Off to the right, an open kitchen hugged the far side of the same room.

They stepped toward the picture windows and onto a light-lavender rug that allowed only a small border of hardwood floor to peek out from underneath. A table in the middle of the room looked to be mahogany, with matching chairs. Beyond that, a low bookcase divided the room nicely, and on the other side, an off-white designer couch with charcoal pillows seemed to be in a comfortable conversation with two plum armchairs and a low-slung mahogany coffee table. Two standing lamps provided more ambient light than reading light but suffused the room with an inviting glow.

As she scanned the room, she paused briefly at each painting hanging on the walls. Obviously Brenna had some incredible pieces, probably from artists she not only knew but had exhibited. And then she saw her own stained-glass window, hanging in front of one of the large picture windows.

Her heart thumped harder knowing that her work had a coveted space in Brenna's life. She couldn't wait to see it in the daylight when the sun's rays filtered through the glass and cast colors across Brenna's floor and furniture.

"You have a beautiful home." Sinclair turned to Brenna and pulled her close.

"Thank you." She kissed her sweetly and Sinclair's shoulders relaxed a bit. She hadn't realized they'd been tense until they loosened, leaving a slight ache when she moved. She cupped the sides of Brenna's face. "I'm still just a little nervous."

"Tell me what you need."

Sinclair took a deep breath. "Nothing, really. Except to be with you."

Brenna smiled broadly. "I'm not going anywhere. I'm taking the day off tomorrow so I'm all yours."

"That's good."

Then Brenna took her hand and led her down a short hall to her bedroom, where she placed Sinclair's suitcase on a wooden chest at the foot of the bed. "The bed's all yours. I'm sleeping on the couch so just let me know if you need any—"

Sinclair put her arms around Brenna and tilted her head toward the bed. "We can both stay here."

"Are you sure?" Brenna's expression was serious but so considerate it warmed Sinclair.

Sinclair nodded. It would be okay.

Brenna excused herself to the kitchen while Sinclair took her toiletry bag to the bathroom that sat off the bedroom.

She was amazed at how well the day had gone. Though much larger than she had imagined it would be, New York was Brenna's town, and her considerateness with every decision that day helped Sinclair feel less nervous.

The clunk of a wooden drawer meant Brenna had returned to the bedroom. Sinclair finished in the bathroom and opened the door.

Brenna held some clothing and pointed to the bathroom. "Do you have everything you need? Just help yourself in there."

"I do." Sinclair paused, then offered Brenna the bathroom with a wave of her hand. "Your turn."

Brenna began to pass her and stopped. "How's the temperature? I can turn the heat on."

"It's just right."

"Would you like a glass of water?"

"No, thanks, I'm fine."

"A different kind of pillow? Those are goose down but I have some—"

"Are you nervous?"

Brenna's shoulders dropped slightly. "I am. I just want you to feel comfortable."

"This is all perfect."

"Yeah?"

"Yeah."

"I'll…I'll be right out, then," Brenna said and stepped into the bathroom.

Sinclair slipped between the silky, clean sheets of the king-size platform bed. Though she was tired from the drive, she was wide-awake, listening to Brenna brush her teeth and wash her hands or face. She was about to spend the night with a new woman. It didn't happen often, but when it had, the pace was usually more rushed and frenetic, almost out of desperation.

It was as if her dates could sense that she might change her mind and run, which was exactly why Sinclair sometimes rushed. They knew it and she knew it.

Not so with Brenna. They had only kissed, and those kisses were magnificently languid and unhurried, making them much more meaningful. A slow kiss demanded true connection and intimacy. It was like sharing a private secret so important that the recipient felt like the giver had entrusted her with its deeply held meaning.

Brenna emerged from the bathroom and stood in the doorway wearing a thin white T-shirt and blue boxer shorts. Sinclair's body immediately reacted to her perfectly sized breasts and long legs. She sucked in an open-mouthed breath and suppressed a groan.

Brenna looked down and then back up and said, "I'm not a regular at Victoria's Secret."

Sinclair chuckled. "Come here anyway."

Brenna slipped into bed. As she lifted the covers revealing Sinclair's white T-shirt and black bikini underwear, Sinclair added, "Neither am I."

"Oh, my God," Brenna whispered. "You're beautiful."

Sinclair opened her arms and Brenna moved into them, tucking her head close to hers, and wrapped her arm over Sinclair's waist. They talked for a long while about Sinclair's drive to New York and Brenna's upcoming show. As they shared stories, Brenna's hand gripped her when she emphasized a certain word, and Sinclair liked the connection. Slowly, she began to rub small circles and ventured to the area between her side and back. Sinclair tried not to flinch when Brenna eventually found the bumps on her skin, but she must have grown stiff because Brenna lifted her head.

"Does that hurt?"

"No." Sinclair had known this conversation would come eventually.

Brenna peered over Sinclair's side and saw the raised circles that dotted her side and back.

"They're cigarette burns," Sinclair said.

"Oh, my God, Sinclair."

"I told you my childhood wasn't very much fun."

Brenna raised up farther and moved over her body. She slowly bent lower to kiss each scar. "This should never have happened to you."

Sinclair closed her eyes as the soft lips soothed her. "I used to wish they'd eventually fade, but it doesn't look like they will."

"If they're a part of you now, then let them represent your strength."

"Sometimes I don't feel too strong."

A powerful mix of tenderness and intensity washed over Brenna's face. "You survived it all."

Deeply moved, Sinclair pulled her into an embrace and held on tight.

"Mmm." Brenna's breath tickled her neck.

It was quiet for a while and Sinclair listened to the faint sounds of the city eighteen stories below. Finally she said, "You have a very huggy family."

Brenna pulled her head back so she could look into Sinclair's eyes. "I know. I hope that's all right. We've always been that way."

"It's wonderful. I'm just not used to it."

"Well, there's nothing like a good hug from Mom to make things feel better. And she'll have a lot of them for you, too."

Sinclair's throat tightened at such a kind and caring offer. Her breath stuttered as she inhaled and Brenna squeezed her tighter.

"I'm sorry for whatever happened to you," Brenna said.

"It was a long time ago."

"But it still hurts."

She was right. The discomfort came up when she let herself be close to people. Maybe that's why she'd always rushed through intimacy before. That way, it was easier to keep the pain at bay. She could get her bodily needs met but stop short of establishing relationships that she was afraid to trust.

"My childhood wasn't a learning ground for family closeness," she said.

She didn't even know how healthy relationships looked. "What was it like growing up in your family?"

Brenna rolled onto her back and reached for Sinclair's hand. "Normal, I guess. We went to school every day and had dinner at home every night, then did our homework. We spent Christmas, Easter, all the holidays, together, or sometimes we'd travel to my mom's only sister's house in Rochester. My mom and dad's parents had all died before I was six, and Dad is an only child, so we spent time with Aunt Alice. We vacationed every summer. Mom and Dad picked different places, but we'd always load up the car and take road trips. My favorites were Arizona, Florida, and California."

"Warm places."

"Absolutely."

"And you and Beanie are close."

"We are now. We didn't used to be. I'm six years older so having a baby sister around didn't work for me sometimes. Imagine trying to impress your high-school friends when your eleven-year-old sister is making stupid slurping noises with her milk shake. And when she graduated from high school, she didn't go to college for a few years and just sat around, goofing off. I'd go over to my parents' house and see her laying around. I didn't like it and we argued a lot. She's so much more laid-back than I am. I thought she should go straight to college like I did, and she thought I had a stick up my ass."

Sinclair nudged her with her hip. "Type A?"

"I suppose I better embrace that. But she's just different than I am and I finally let it go. She's an amazing person. I love her to death."

She loves her to death. The thought made Sinclair uneasy.

"My dad is a developer and my mom works for the county records department. We all get together at least once a week for dinner. Beanie's got a boyfriend who's nice. I'd say I've had a pretty easy life. It's all pretty normal stuff."

"Normal is nice."

"Are you in contact with your stepbrother?"

"No. I imagine he's still abusive and I had enough back then."

She heard Brenna inhale deeply and blow her breath out. What could she tell her? It was bad enough that she'd risked everything to come to New York, consequently exposing herself, but could she trust Brenna?

No, not yet. "When I left, I cut all ties. I haven't spoken to him since and that's the way it needs to be."

"You're a strong woman for escaping. Leaving at fifteen must have been so scary. And hard on you." She raised up, turning toward Sinclair, supporting herself on her elbow. "I've never had to struggle for anything. I've been fortunate to have my family. They provided me with everything I needed."

"What about love?"

"Struggle for love? I can't say that I have, really. I've had some girlfriends," she said, then paused. "Sure, lies and betrayals and arguments were difficult, but it was always easier to leave a relationship than to fight for something. I mean, by the time the shit hit the fan, the emotional connection was usually pretty much destroyed."

"When was your last relationship?"

"A long time ago. I was with a woman named Petra for about a year. She was an artist. It was good for a while but then it went to hell."

"What happened?"

"I fell really hard for her. She was a controlling person and I let her be. So much so that I neglected my gallery. We stayed in her apartment day and night, living off sushi, wine, and what I thought was love. The business virtually fell into ruins. I wasn't going in or paying bills, and Lucy, who was my only employee at the time, floundered while I rolled around in my irresponsibility.

"My parents funded the opening of the gallery, and they got wind of all that and stepped in. It was completely embarrassing, failing my mom and dad like that. Default notices started rolling in, but I still didn't care. My mom harangued me but I fought back, saying I was an adult and could tend to my life as I wanted.

"And then one evening, my phone rang. I could hear Petra talking with another woman, and though the conversation was muffled, I could tell it was pretty intimate."

"She called you to let you know she was with another woman?"

"Not exactly. She butt-dialed me and I heard more than I wanted to. When I confronted her, she told me she felt trapped and wanted to see other people. I was devastated and left her. After that, I focused only on my business and finally brought it back from ruination. If I hadn't gotten that phone call, I'd have lost the gallery."

"Wow. I guess it was better to find out sooner than later."

"Yeah. I owe my undying gratitude to her butt."

She laughed at Brenna's ability to recover. "And since then?"

"Nothing but work."

"You haven't seen anyone?"

"I've dated. Mostly artists, though you'd think I would have learned that lesson, but since my social circle revolves around them, that's who I meet. I've never had a long-term relationship, though."

"Why do you think that is?"

"I don't know. It's a lot of work sometimes. More work than the gallery. When I date someone, we have some fun, and then it ends. I'm not sure I'm the staying type."

"The staying type?"

"Dating's the easy part. But after a while, I can't picture myself with them for the long haul. Or if we start to fight, it's been easier to leave. Other than Petra, maybe that's why I've never had a bad breakup to speak of."

"No one's ever tried to fight for you?"

"A little, maybe. But I could never give them as much as they wanted. Since Petra, I haven't let anything get between me and my work, so I've been accused of being callous and selfish."

"Do you think you're those things?"

Brenna was quiet for a moment. "I don't think I'm callous. When I've broken up with someone, I'm sure it looked like I didn't care, but to them the only way I could appear to care for them is if I stayed with them. Which I couldn't do once I felt it was over. And I imagine that walking away from a relationship because I was done would make me selfish."

"What kind of relationship would be right for you?"

"That's a good question. I want to find something with that person that makes me want to stay. Something that would really keep me there. But sometimes I wonder if I haven't gotten to the place where I leave before I can ever find out."

"Artists can be difficult people."

Brenna smiled. "Don't I know it."

"So, is that why you like me?"

"I like passion. Artists wear their hearts on their sleeves and it's sexy. But with you, it feels like more than that. I know that must sound like a line, but," she slowly shook her head as if she were pleasantly surprised, "I felt immediately drawn to you on a more emotional level."

"Even though I almost scared you off?"

She chuckled. "After I realized you weren't going to clock me on the head with a rock or something, I wasn't too scared. I know we're just getting to know each other, but this feels really different than what I've experienced with other women. Does that sound weird?"

"Not at all. Except for the rock part. If I didn't feel the same way, you couldn't have convinced me to leave Pemaquid Point."

"I'm glad, then." Brenna smiled, and the sultry look in her eyes felt like an aphrodisiac. Sinclair's chest grew warm.

"What about you?" Brenna said.

"I'm not overly experienced in the relationship department. The only one that was mildly serious was with a woman in town. Well, all have been with women in town."

Brenna's eyes widened playfully.

"I mean, there've only been a few. I don't get out much. Donna and I were together on and off for a few years, but I decided we were better friends than lovers."

"Donna...the bartender at the Seaside Stop?"

"Yeah. Do you know her?"

"I stopped in the day after we first met. Great crab cakes."

"Yes. And she's great, too. I'm glad we're best friends now."

"And the others?"

"Just some women who live locally. A dinner here and there but nothing serious."

Brenna reached over to her cheek and stroked it gently. "I like you, Sinclair Grady."

Brenna's comment allowed her to inhale deeply and let out an excited breath. In the couple of weeks since meeting Brenna, she'd busied herself making arrangements for the trip and picked up the pace on her work. She'd mostly worried about leaving her safe haven and how she'd feel once she was in the city. Even during the long drive south, she envisioned different scenarios in a city full of hazards, mentally rehearsing how to stay calm and not look over her shoulder.

What she hadn't anticipated hit her like a rogue wave when she walked into the L'Art de Vie Gallery and saw the broad smile on Brenna's lovely face. An unbelievably strong and immediate desire for Brenna had erupted inside her and threatened to buckle her knees.

"I like you, too, Brenna Wright."

Brenna pulled her closer, and Sinclair kissed her. Brenna's soft lips responded to hers and their tongues met in earnest discovery. The kiss was deeper, more sensuous than before. Brenna was tender, delicate, and extremely considerate of her feelings. Brenna wanted her to feel comfortable, and though it was obvious that their feelings for each other were progressing, she was taking things slow, which was incredibly sexy.

After a long while, Sinclair pulled away slowly. "You're a remarkable kisser."

"Takes one to know one." Brenna balanced on one elbow, looking down at her. "I love your lips." She brushed a finger over them.

Sinclair wanted to purr. "I can't remember the last time I made out for so long."

"I can't remember the last time I heard the term *made out*."

They laughed and Sinclair said, "I know it sounds like high school, but I feel like an excited teenager right now."

"So do I. This is awesome. I could kiss you all night."

Sinclair inhaled slowly and sighed. "You'd stop if I needed you to, wouldn't you?"

"I would, yes." Brenna's eyes sparkled.

"Thank you for being so understanding."

"You've taken a big step by coming here to see me. Whatever makes you feel comfortable and safe, Sinclair, I'll do. Or not do. Just let me know what you need."

"What do *you* need?"

"You being here. As far as what I want, I want to spend time with you. I want to take things one at a time, if that's what will give us the best chance of getting to know each other." Sinclair watched Brenna's lips. "I want to please you."

"Define *please*."

Brenna looked as if she was trying to squash a smile. "I knew that might get me into trouble as soon as the word left my mouth. I want what pleases you. I want you to have a great time while you're here. I'm not necessarily referring to while we're in my bed."

Sinclair felt so at ease she couldn't help but tease her a little. "Not necessarily?"

"Well, I'm not sure what you want so I don't want to be presumptuous."

"You're being very chivalrous right now."

"It's hard to lie here and be well-mannered without part of my brain screaming that I've got an unbelievably stunning woman in bed with me right now."

"Am I making this difficult for you?"

"Very."

"Do you want to make out some more?"

Steamy-sultry ardor flashed in Brenna's eyes. Sinclair pulled Brenna on top of her.

She eagerly welcomed her mouth and tongue as Brenna kissed her with languid, easy strokes of her tongue and quick teasing nips at Sinclair's lips. They explored each other thoroughly, intimately, and the more they took their time learning each other with their mouths, the more Sinclair got turned on.

She wanted Brenna's hands all over her, rubbing and grabbing and searching, and her deliberateness and slow pace were driving her crazy. When Brenna gently bit her lip, Sinclair's skin tingled and she groaned. She caressed Brenna's side, along her arm. A rush of excitement raced through her as Brenna shifted, exposing her breast to Sinclair's touch.

Sinclair inched her hand up until her fingers brushed over a hard nipple. Brenna shuddered in response and kissed her harder.

Heat seared between Sinclair's legs, and the thought of going slowly and gently flew out of her brain. She sucked Brenna's tongue, drawing her deeper inside.

Her body ignited under Brenna's. She felt the hardness of Brenna's thighs, tasted the sweet saltiness of her neck, and heard the rapid breathing of their arousal. Her own thighs ached to engulf Brenna so she opened them and wrapped them around her.

Sinclair broke the kiss after what seemed like forever. Brenna was letting her take the lead, letting her set the pace. Her stomach tightened as the lust that raged inside her and every touch from Brenna became sweet agony.

The need to feed that lust sent her hands to Brenna's ass and she opened her legs and pulled her closer, driving Brenna's hips between her open legs. Brenna broke their kiss and dropped her head into Sinclair's neck, moaning loudly.

In that moment, everything felt right. She wouldn't think about the short time she'd known Brenna or whether things were advancing too quickly. Right then she wanted to be close to her, to feel her and move with her. She wanted to hear more of the intimate sounds she made when she was aroused.

"Sin...clair," she said, gasping. "Don't do that."

The plea seemed to be less of a warning than a revelation of Brenna's own desperate hold on her control.

She didn't stop. "I need to feel you."

Brenna moaned again, pressing harder against Sinclair. When she raised up on her hands, her hair fell softly over Sinclair's face. Brenna rocked side to side between her legs, and when her eyebrows rose slightly, the look of ecstasy signaled she had located the spot where her clit had the best contact. And when she found it, she began to glide up and down in unhurried strokes.

Sinclair whispered, "Yes."

❖

Brenna wanted her desperately. When Sinclair spread her legs and pulled her down on top of her, hot tremors of arousal slammed into her, shredding her willpower. Now she couldn't control her need. She had to come soon or she'd go crazy.

Her clit fit between Sinclair's legs perfectly, and even with the barrier of her boxers, she was amazingly hard.

The slow thrusts against Sinclair's pelvic bone sent a roiling torrent through her body, and she went with the delirious sensation and relinquished all reason. She brushed her mouth over Sinclair's ear. "I can't go slowly any more."

"Good."

"Oh, God, are you sure?" She was so close to climaxing, she could hardly think.

"Yes. Just don't stop."

"We…" It was so hard to talk. "We…still have…our clothes on."

"Don't stop."

Brenna could only gulp air in quick gasps as her heart hammered and her clit burned for release. Wetness soaked her underwear and thighs.

"Oh, God," she whimpered, unable to stop even if the building had collapsed around them.

Sinclair clutched her ass, guiding her.

Brenna arched up, trying to prolong the feeling of Sinclair under her and to keep her orgasm at bay, but Sinclair's lips found her breast, sucking gently but firmly on her nipple.

"Sinclair…" She wanted to plead for mercy or apologize for losing control, not sure which Sinclair needed most. "I'm sorr—"

Sinclair grabbed her head, pulling her back down. "I want you to come for me."

Brenna fell off the edge she'd been desperately clinging to and came hard. She cried out and held on to Sinclair's shoulders as the waves kept rolling through her.

"Come for me," Sinclair whispered. "Don't stop."

Brenna surrendered to the glorious ride, the spasms lasting even longer as she pressed herself to Sinclair's body.

When the contractions stopped, she pushed her clit firmly against Sinclair. All she could think about was Sinclair's body and her mouth and the things she'd said. The memory of Sinclair asking her to come for her caused another slightly less intense wave to pulse fervently between her legs. The new ripples surprised her and she groaned loudly.

When her second orgasm subsided, she tried to shift away but Sinclair held her there.

"Stay," she said.

Brenna relaxed, her whole body settling into mush as Sinclair stroked and kissed her hair.

CHAPTER FOURTEEN

B renna awoke alone in bed. She was still in her T-shirt and boxer shorts, which made her chuckle. Throwing off the covers, she made contact with the cool, slate floor and walked to the living room. Sinclair stood at the window, staring out over the city. Dawn had come recently and the buildings glowed with the first emergence of the sun.

"Good morning," Brenna said as she wrapped her arms around Sinclair from behind.

"Hi."

"If you look down there to the right of the green awning on the corner, you'll be able to see a line forming at one of the best coffee houses in the city."

When Sinclair didn't respond, Brenna said, "Are you all right?"

"Do you sometimes wonder what would happen if everything changed?"

"Everything? Like in a good way?" She hugged her tighter.

"No. If everything came crashing down."

Puzzled, Brenna said, "What do you mean?"

Sinclair turned to face her. "Nothing."

"No, really, what do you mean?"

"It must be the view from this high. Seriously, it was nothing."

It was a strange question but Sinclair seemed to shrug it off as inconsequential.

"Do you have any coffee?"

"I do! It's from that corner place. Let me make some."

From the kitchen, Brenna watched Sinclair step back and sit on the couch, still taking in the view out the window. She didn't seem to want to talk so Brenna busied herself with the coffee press.

She'd gotten quiet at dinner, too. Maybe she was just a little overwhelmed. She probably wasn't used to being around a chatty family.

But as lighthearted as the family was, Brenna's mother had still found a way to give her the eye. It was that familiar look that meant, "Are you getting into another relationship with someone that will take you away from your business?" Brenna's Pavlovian response to take heed, like she had so many times before, was strong. She knew she'd have to face a stern discussion with her parental unit at some point, but right now, she just wanted to be with Sinclair.

❖

Brenna took her to Balthazar in SoHo. Sinclair had never been to a French bistro and was delighted to absorb the atmosphere. They sat in a red leather banquette under an antique yellow ceiling. The retro stained mirrors multiplied the movements of the diners, creating a bold, loud, and exhilarating ambience.

"Try this." Brenna held out her fork, laden with sour cream and hazelnut waffles and warm berries.

The sensation was nothing short of exquisite. Sinclair shared her buckwheat crepe, making sure Brenna had a large forkful of eggs, ham, and Gruyère cheese.

She smiled as broadly as Brenna, enjoying a sunny morning in the city. They had slept in, though Sinclair's body clock woke her briefly at four. Today she would do no low-tide scavenging and enjoy nothing but Brenna's company.

Sharing Brenna's bed hadn't been uncomfortable or strange. They cuddled through the night and Sinclair felt protected in her arms.

"May I admit something?" Brenna held her coffee cup and looked completely edible.

"Sure."

Lowering her voice, she said, "I've never come with my clothes on."

Sinclair looked up at the ceiling, not sure whether to be embarrassed. "Was that a bad thing?"

Brenna reached for her hand. "No. Not at all. It surprised me but I loved it."

"So did I."

"I wish I could have…returned the favor."

Sinclair pushed the last of her crepe around on the plate. "I just wanted to hold you after that."

"And that was perfect," Brenna said. "But did we go a little too far?"

"No. I couldn't have stopped if I'd tried, which I didn't. Part of me wanted to take it slow and the rest of me was going nuts. I think what happened was amazing. And sexy."

"It was, wasn't it?" Brenna smiled and took a sip of coffee. "Having so little skin contact was somehow really hot. I never thought I'd say that, but with you, it rocked me senseless."

"I was pretty turned on, too." Sinclair felt more alive than she'd ever known. Her spirit soared with possibilities.

"It just makes me want you more."

"Well, it's decided, then."

"More?"

"Yes, more."

❖

They walked through the Canal Street neighborhood, talking and browsing the wares of the open storefronts and street vendors.

"This neighborhood was once called Hell's Hundred Acres. This was where the sweatshops and small industrial factories used to be." Brenna pointed as she talked. "Sometime around the mid-1900s artists began to move into these abandoned buildings and took up residence in the upper stories. They called them lofts, and the artists loved them because they were cheap, large areas with high ceilings and lots of natural light."

Sinclair could see why artists wanted to live in the neighborhood. The architecture and signage were eclectic and fostered imaginative thinking.

"There's a place I think you'd like." They walked the few blocks up West Broadway and turned down Price Street. Halfway down the block, Brenna stopped her and turned her toward a building across the street.

"Look up," she said.

There, in a large window, hung one of her sea-glass pieces.

"My God," she said, astonished to see her work already in New York.

"That's how I found you. I know the artist who lives there."

From behind, Brenna wrapped her arms around her and Sinclair reached down to hold her wrists.

"That's so cool." She felt the giddiness of a child being told she was going to Disneyland.

"It is. And I'm glad I went by and saw it. It led me to you."

Sinclair leaned her head back and felt Brenna's face snuggling close to her ear. "I'm so glad you're here," Brenna said.

Sinclair turned around and kissed her. She was, too.

❖

They walked down 6th Avenue and down 4th Street to Washington Square Park.

There, Brenna pointed out the Washington Arch and a large fountain populated by lunch eaters and mothers with children while a fire eater competed for "loose change" with a couple on unicycles. There were also children's play areas full of blurred little ones running about and a chess and Scrabble area with players of every type and age.

They came out of the park and onto University Place, where they walked a number of blocks to the Union Square Park and entered a vast place called the Greenmarket.

The farmers' market was busy with vendors and customers buying everything from organic fruit and vegetables to meats and cheeses. Cut flowers, jams, and artisan bread vendors rubbed elbows with chef demonstrations and recycling organizations.

They ate a light lunch there and then Brenna bought ice-cream cones. They found a bench and sat down, enjoying the sun and watching the passersby.

"How do you like New York so far?" Brenna said.

Sinclair licked a drip of chocolate that was making its way down her cone, trying to reach her hand. "This is great. I have a wonderful tour guide."

"Are you tired from walking?"

"No, not yet. But if you plan to walk back to your place, I have no idea if we're a block away or five miles."

"We can take a taxi any time you'd like. But I want you to see one more place before we get back. And I hope it's okay that we're having dinner with Beanie and Pete, her boyfriend."

"I'd like that." How refreshing it was to see siblings interact with love and respect. She'd never experienced the same with her stepbrother. The loving interaction of the Wright family seemed a bit surreal, but it was her own upbringing that had been strange. Horrible, actually.

She wanted to spend time with the people who loved Brenna and knew her well. She wanted to know all about how healthy relationships worked.

❖

They stayed in Union Square Park until the sun started to set. A chilly breeze enveloped them so Brenna hailed a taxi to their next destination. It was Sinclair's first taxi ride, and Brenna held her hand as the driver swerved in and out of traffic, barely avoiding a few accidents, or so Sinclair was convinced.

They finally arrived at 30 Rockefeller Plaza, an extremely tall building on 50th Street between 5th and 6th Avenues. Brenna retrieved some tickets from her pocket and they boarded an elevator to the 70th floor, which turned out to be the top level.

An open-air terrace encircled the building, providing a breathtaking and unobstructed 360-degree view of New York City and beyond.

As they walked around each side, Brenna pointed out stunning views of Brooklyn, New Jersey, and Liberty Island. "There's Central Park," Brenna said, indicating the largest park Sinclair had ever seen. And when she showed her the Empire State Building, Brenna said, "Most people go there for the view, but I think this one far exceeds it."

The panorama far exceeded anything Sinclair had ever experienced, that was for sure. She was on top of the world, with a sexy woman offering her the grandeur of the Big Apple.

"John D. Rockefeller built all this as a gift to the people of New York. When the Great Depression hit and so many people were unemployed, he decided to move forward with his plans anyway and gave thousands of men and women jobs. For the next nine years, those people had food on their table because of his love for the city."

As a chilly wind whipped up over the edge of the observation terrace, Sinclair took her hand and they continued gazing out over the awe-inspiring vista.

"What are you thinking about?" Brenna said.

"How I might have never seen New York if I hadn't met you. I was thinking about our morning, just walking around, and how great it feels to be with you."

Brenna turned toward her and wrapped her arms around her. "Kiss me before I wake up and realize you're just a fantastic dream."

Sinclair could never tire of Brenna's soft lips. The swirly little flutters that erupted inside her each time their lips met came again, and she almost smiled in the middle of the kiss.

"This is no dream."

"Good," Brenna said. "Because I'm never able to yell when I'm asleep." She turned toward the Empire State building and let out a whoop that made Sinclair laugh.

"Yup, this is really happening." Brenna kissed her again. "I've got the most insane crush on you. All I can think about is that I'll go mad when you leave to go back to Maine."

There was that, Sinclair thought, her joy deflating slightly. She would return home and then come back for the exhibition, but where could this relationship really go?

"I guess there are some tricky logistics."

"Like how I'm going to wear my tires out driving up to see you continuously? Or racking up enough frequent-flier miles to redeem them for expensive luggage or whatever they offer?"

"Maybe it's too soon to talk about it."

Brenna lowered her head a couple of inches so her eyes were level with Sinclair's. "I don't think it is, but if you're feeling pressured, just let me know and I'll back off."

"It's just that I hadn't even considered dating anyone for a long time, let alone someone who lives in another state."

"You're right. Let's just take things one at a time, then. I mean, you don't even know any of my character flaws yet."

"What are they?"

"The Top of the Rock will close long before I could get them all out."

"Okay. Just name two."

Brenna looked out over the view and her mouth curled into a smile. "Other than being a type A?"

"Yes. We've already established that so it doesn't count."

"Well, maybe this is a subset of that, but sometimes I'm like a bull in a china shop."

"How so?"

"I don't take time to consider the whole picture. When I want something, I usually just charge in. And that can cause problems."

"Like what?"

"I can offend people or make them feel rushed into a decision."

"And then what happens?"

"I can usually work through things. Like I said before, I don't think I've really struggled for anything."

"Okay. So, what's the other character flaw?"

Brenna seemed to get a little more serious. Her smile drooped and then stretched into pursed lips. "Just what I said. That I've never really struggled for anything." A gust of wind blew in behind Sinclair, and Brenna reached up to move a lock of hair from her eyes. Sinclair loved how her fingers felt against her skin. "I don't think I'm a very strong person. You can't look at someone's accomplishments to make that determination. You have to look at their hardships and the times they've had to grapple and tussle for something they believed in. I haven't lived through anything like that."

"Maybe that's fortunate."

"I don't know how I'd do with a really big problem in life, you know? I feel as if I've been skating along on thick, smooth ice with nothing in my way. But I don't know what's ahead and how I'd do if it really got rough."

"I wouldn't say that's a character flaw."

"Flaws aren't always known. They can be unknown."

She looked at Sinclair with an expression that seemed so vulnerable, like a small child would look if susceptible to exposure.

Sinclair pulled her into a bear hug. Brenna hugged back and they remained silent for a while, as the sounds of the city reverberated on the walls around them. Sinclair knew she was falling for her. She let her heart absorb this moment, knowing that incredible things might happen between them. Brenna was real and true and humbly magnificent. "Thank you for telling me."

"I'd say thank you for not running away from me, but you don't know how to get back to your car at the gallery."

Sinclair pushed her playfully and Brenna wrapped her arm around her, turning her toward the elevator.

"Come on, dinner awaits."

Chapter Fifteen

Brenna continued her role as tour guide, pointing out interesting places to Sinclair as they traveled to Hell's Kitchen to meet Beanie and her boyfriend for dinner. Sinclair had never eaten Thai food before, so when they walked into Pam Real Thai, eccentric aromas hit her nose. She detected a mix of onion, lemongrass, and garlic, but also wafts of some type of chili sauce or other peppers that made her stomach grumble for attention.

They sat in the back room, under a large portrait of a woman who was the restaurant's namesake as well as the same person that greeted them at the door. The place wasn't fancy—more like a cafeteria with a tile floor and no-nonsense chair and tables. The décor was Asian in style with a hodgepodge of pictures decorated with old Christmas ornaments.

Beanie and her boyfriend came in just after they sat, and Brenna hugged them both and turned to Sinclair. "You remember Beanie and this is Pete."

She shook his hand and noticed that it was very soft for a guy. She was used to the rough, calloused hands of fishermen when she went to the docks to get a fresh catch for dinner.

"Okay," Brenna said when they all sat down. "This is Sinclair's first time to eat Thai."

"How fun!" Beanie opened her menu. "Some people describe it as being similar to Chinese food but with a sting, though it depends on what you order."

"I'll let you order for me, then," Sinclair said as she looked through her menu and perused dishes like Fried Taro Dumpling and Tom Yum Soup. "It all looks pretty exotic."

Brenna placed her hand on Sinclair's thigh and squeezed. "You're a trooper."

"I suppose Thai food is known most for balancing sour, sweet, and salty flavors, and then throwing in a little heat," Pete said. "It's as complex or as simple as you want."

Brenna and Beanie ordered for the table, and when the dishes arrived, everything looked delectable. She tried glass noodle soup, green curry, something called larb, and an interesting noodle dish called Pad Key Mao, that mixed the flavors of basil, onion, and chili.

They talked through dinner about life in New York, how Beanie met Pete, what their parents were doing for their vacation, and other wonderfully mundane family topics. It was nice to watch Brenna and Beanie interact with the familiarity developed while growing up together. The loving trust and history between them seemed solid and enviably strong. Sinclair could tell Pete had probably already come to the same conclusion because he smiled warmly and remained very attentive to Beanie.

"Where did you get the name Beanie?" Sinclair asked when the waiter came for their plates.

Brenna loved the way Sinclair both listened and joined the talk, even though a lot of it dealt with tales of the Wright family. Her profile was exquisite, and watching her as she talked to Beanie and Pete allowed Brenna time to take in her beautiful smile and perfect nose.

"My nickname? Oh, it was from an unfortunate occurrence when I was three. I found a bag of Mom's lima beans in the cabinet and decided to eat them."

"But what she didn't know," Brenna said, "was they were raw, which made them poisonous."

"So what happened?"

"Mom found her right away and got the mush out of her mouth but didn't know how much she'd swallowed. She had to take her to the emergency room to get her stomach pumped."

Pete nodded casually. "Nice."

"That's horrible."

"What was really bad," Brenna said, "was that after they went through all that, they found out she hadn't swallowed anything."

Beanie shook her head. "I was three, what did I know?"

"So after that, when she got close to the cabinet, I'd always hear mom saying to her, 'No beans, honey, no beans.'"

"And Brenna decided to call me Beanie."

"What's your real name?"

"Ivory."

"I like Beanie better," Pete said.

Beanie laughed. "So do I."

Pete's cell phone chirped. He read the text and said, "I've gotta get going." He jumped up and fished some money out of his wallet. Giving it to Beanie, he kissed her and said, "I'll call you later, babe."

He took Sinclair's hand, "It was really nice meeting you. I can see you're very special. Brenna doesn't let us meet her dates very often." He winked at her and left.

"Pete's a resident in anesthesiology at New York Presbyterian."

That explained the soft hands. "He seems very sweet."

"He is," Brenna said. "Otherwise, I'd kill him." Beanie laughed but Sinclair looked as if she'd bitten into a chili pepper. She winced, then recovered with a thin smile.

"Are you okay?"

"I'm fine," Sinclair said, then turned to Beanie. "He's very nice. And so are you. You have a lovely family."

"I haven't seen Brenna this giddy since her high-school prom."

"I wasn't giddy," Brenna said. "I was drunk." She turned to Sinclair. "But I am truly happy right now."

It seemed that she had said something wrong because even though Sinclair had said she was all right, her mood had shifted. Her body had tensed in that barely discernible way someone would if they had just gotten a chill.

She turned to her a few times, looking into her eyes, inviting an openness that said, "If you want to talk about it, I'm right here."

But Sinclair just squeezed her hand or smiled before returning to the conversation at hand.

They paid their tab and bid Beanie good-bye before hailing a taxi back to Brenna's place.

CHAPTER SIXTEEN

At the large bedroom window, Sinclair stood in nothing but a T-shirt and underwear, watching the nighttime rhythm of the city below. With the lights out in the bedroom, the view was crisp and almost surreal. Vehicles moved north and south like red and white blood cells as they pulsed through each traffic light. Signs glowed along the streets and boulevards, some blinking on and off as if ticking off the minutes until dawn when they would shut off and rest. Rooftops below were too obscure in the night for her to see many details of them, and most of the windows of other apartments were either shaded or dark. Some flickered from what was probably a television, but otherwise the tenants seemed to be sleeping or were out for the night.

She heard Brenna come out of the bathroom and closed her eyes in anticipation. When she felt arms envelop her, she let her head rest on Brenna's shoulder.

As Brenna kissed her ear, Sinclair luxuriated in the lips that she was beginning to covet. Brenna moved down to her neck, and she raised her head off Brenna and dropped her chin toward her chest. Brenna kissed and licked the back of her neck along the line of her T-shirt and moved her hands lightly up toward her breasts and then down, all the way to her thighs. When she felt the firm, commanding grip of Brenna's hands on her hips, she erupted in tingles.

Sinclair reached out with both hands, placing them on the window for support, and as she leaned forward, Brenna's body molded into hers.

Brenna's hands and lips were so languid and deliberate, Sinclair felt extremely sexy and desirable. Like a relaxing dream that comes slowly and wonderfully, she fell into the sensations Brenna stirred within and welcomed the light-headed feeling of pleasure. For a long while, Brenna explored her body and massaged, stroked, and tended to everything she could reach from where they stood spooning.

At one point, Brenna balanced herself by reaching out for the window and placing her palm close to Sinclair's hand. She watched Brenna's arm muscles flex. The mermaid tattoo undulated slightly, which was so sexy she couldn't help the desire that burned inside her. She needed for this hot, assertive woman to take her over.

Brenna ran her other hand under her T-shirt and Sinclair allowed her to lift it off. As soon as her shirt dropped to the floor, the tattooed arm withdrew and she felt more than saw Brenna remove her shirt as well. She gasped as she felt warm flesh return, hugging her back.

Soon, both pairs of underwear were off and Sinclair was still leaning against the window with her hands up against it again for support. She was partially aware that though the lights were off, someone might be able to see them up against the window, but the rest of the world seemed miles away. The movement of the traffic and the blinking lights seemed like a pretend city with toy buildings and little plastic people.

She didn't care. She didn't care about anything but Brenna.

Brenna's breasts pressed against her back and felt hot and alive. Brenna stroked the front of her thigh then cupped her breast. And when Brenna inched her hand down, over Sinclair's stomach and then between her legs, she opened wider, as though being frisked.

She took one hand from the glass and wrapped it behind her to grip Brenna's ass just as strong fingers slid inside her.

She gasped and Brenna replied with a moan.

Sinclair was high, tumbling into the kind of full-tilt drunken stupor that only came from being filled up with the slowly plunging fingers of a woman.

They moved together to the cadence of Brenna's hand. Sinclair met each thrust, taking Brenna as deeply as she could, and they rocked back and forth until Sinclair felt the tingling precursor of an orgasm.

It began at the base of her spine, a swirling sensation that traveled simultaneously up her legs and down her back. The slurping noise her wetness made against Brenna's hand and the feel of Brenna's hot, straining fingers made her orgasm grow slowly but forcefully until all her senses converged on the point between her legs.

Brenna's fingers relentlessly coaxed her on. Sinclair needed to shift position, to get off her trembling legs, but she couldn't. She was pinned there, unable to move. Her lungs were barely able to function in a struggle to get oxygen. And finally, even they froze as she took in one gulp of air and held it. The room went silent for a nanosecond, then her orgasm crashed upon her as she screamed Brenna's name.

❖

Light, loving lips gently kissed Sinclair's eyes and she opened them to the sight of Brenna snuggled close in bed. Morning sun streamed into the flat, and the constant drone of the urban traffic below them reminded her of the lulling sound of country crickets.

"Good morning," Sinclair said.

"I've been lying here feeling more comfortable than I can remember."

"You have?"

"Mmm," Brenna said. "You like to wrap your legs around your sleeping partner, did you know that?"

"I can't say that I did. I hope I didn't snore or talk in my sleep."

"I'll never tell."

"This does feel good, being here with you." Sinclair's heart felt light knowing that her life could be changing forever. She fit so well with Brenna.

"We have two days left," Brenna said. "Today I'd like to take you through the gallery and really show you around and sign some exhibit paperwork. After that, I plan to take the rest of the time off to be with you. What would you like to do?"

"What do you suggest?"

"We could travel up the Hudson, to upstate New York. It's a beautiful drive. Or we could hang out in the city, maybe see a show or walk around some other boroughs. Of course, there's always eating. We could eat our way through the best tourist stops, if you'd like."

"It all sounds fun." Sinclair looked forward to seeing more of New York through Brenna's eyes. She was the perfect host and an even better lover. "Maybe we could spend some more time right here."

Brenna kissed her. "I admit, that's at the top of my list."

Two more days and she'd be going home. After that, the exhibition would give them the opportunity to see each other again, but then what? Would this relationship be too geographically challenged?

"If you'd asked me a few weeks ago, I never would have thought I'd be saying this, but I don't look forward to going home."

"I don't want you to leave."

"What about the distance between our homes?"

Brenna sat up in bed, crossing her legs. The covers fell around her hips, and sudden desire from the sight of her broad shoulders and shapely breasts made Sinclair inhale sharply.

"Nothing's insurmountable, is it?"

Sinclair felt the familiar twinge of caution about matters she wasn't completely in control of. "We'll see."

"That sounds a bit cryptic."

It was true but maybe she shouldn't have said it. She tried her best to smile through her sudden trepidation. "What do you expect from a difficult artist?"

Chapter Seventeen

They arrived at L'Art de Vie after a breakfast at Daniel's Bagels on 3rd Avenue. Brenna had taken her there because they had the best bagels in New York. She watched with delight as Sinclair tried the dense, chewy jewels and beamed when Sinclair swore she'd never forget the taste.

Brenna paid the taxi driver and they stepped out onto the sidewalk in front of her gallery. "I know I whisked you away the other day, so now we can spend some time looking at the gallery and talking about your exhibition." She took her hand as they walked in.

Lucy looked up from the front desk and smiled. "Hey, you two. I was beginning to wonder when you'd surface again."

"Brenna's been showing me the city."

"And how do you like it?"

"It's big and fantastic and has some of the best food I've ever eaten."

"Well," Lucy said, "we can't rival your lobsters, I'm sure, but we do well with about a million different ethnic cuisines."

Carl glided up. "Now this is the way to add beauty to your gallery, Brenna. Sinclair looks absolutely magnificent."

Sinclair seemed to brighten behind the immediate blush that colored her cheeks. "Thank you."

"It looks like you two are good for each other. Even Brenna looks different." He made a show of walking around her and scrutinizing her, then pointed a finger in the air. "It's love, I believe."

Sinclair's smile looked as happy as Brenna felt inside.

"What's this I hear about love?"

Brenna turned to see Nina Leone standing behind her.

"Nina," Lucy said. "Have you come to see your paintings? They're all hung, darling."

"Actually, I came to see Brenna, but I might have shown up too late." Nina looked directly at Sinclair's hand, which was still holding Brenna's. Her eyes traveled up Sinclair's arm, her body, and stopped to stare at her face.

Brenna moved her hand from Sinclair's and put it protectively around her shoulder. "Nina, I'd like you to meet Sinclair. Sinclair, this is Nina. Some of her pieces are in our next show."

Nina nodded and, to Brenna's amusement, Sinclair nodded back.

"Sinclair is an artist as well, Nina. You own one of her pieces."

Nina's eyes flickered, her brows lowering momentarily, and then she said, "Sinclair Grady. From Maine."

"Was it Nina's place you took me by yesterday?"

Brenna was about to answer but Nina spoke up. "You were that close and didn't stop in? As you remember, we never had our second drink."

"Thank you for buying it," Sinclair said. "It was a thrill to see it in your window,"

"It's beautiful. And so is the artist." Nina looked at Brenna. "But I see Brenna's already figured that out."

"Carl," Brenna said, "would you take care of Nina?" She didn't need her kicking up any more dust. "Nina, will you excuse us?"

Brenna took Sinclair into the next room, and when she turned to talk to her, Sinclair was almost laughing.

"She's got it bad for you."

"Don't remind me."

"Is she your ex?"

"No. We do business together, but I've avoided anything personal."

"So, what if I've got it bad for you?"

Brenna stepped closer. "I'd ask you to remind me more often."

Their kiss was tender and then Brenna hugged Sinclair. "Sorry about that. No one can control her."

"She's an artist, after all."

"But light years different from you."

Brenna showed her the rest of the space and they talked about how to display Sinclair's glass pieces. She wanted to fill the windows with them to capitalize on the sun. They would also install window boxes with lighting behind the pieces that mounted to the walls to allow those glass colors to be illuminated as well.

Nina remained with Carl but kept her eye on the two of them. Brenna didn't like the feeling of her stares, and while Carl would normally relish the drama of a situation such as this, she was relieved that he seemed to try to keep Nina away from them.

They had gone through the entire gallery when Lucy found them in the back room. "Brenna, the transporters are here to unload the Wellington pieces. They need you to inspect the truck contents and sign off before they unload."

"Okay."

"Unfortunately, they're around the block on 76th Street because they couldn't double-park out front."

"I'll be back soon," Brenna said to Sinclair. "Lucy, would you get her a cup of coffee or wine, please?"

"We have white and red," Lucy said as Sinclair followed her to the front desk and pointed to a wine cooler under it. "And coffee or tea."

"Coffee, please."

"It's in the back. Cream? Sugar?"

"Just cream, please."

While Sinclair waited by the front desk, Carl and Nina pointed this way and that as if redesigning the walls, until they moved into the farthest room and out of her sight. For a moment, she was alone in the front of the gallery, but then a woman with curly, blond hair rushed in the front door and hurried toward the back. She hadn't looked up as she passed Sinclair, but at the floor, determined in her movements.

Maybe she was an assistant, late for work.

By herself again, Sinclair took in the entire space. She absolutely loved it and marveled at the business Brenna had created. She was really doing well, and by the look of the shops across the street, the gallery was in a pricey neighborhood.

"Excuse me, ma'am?"

Two large, uniformed police officers had walked up to her, startling her with their imposing presence.

Sinclair's throat suddenly tightened and she couldn't speak.

The tallest officer said, "Ma'am? Do you work here?"

They both stared at her and her heart lurched.

"Ma'am?" the other one said.

She took a fleeting glance toward the front door.

The tall officer looked at the other, then frowned. "Are you going to say anything?"

Panic rose in her chest, stealing the air from her lungs.

The other officer raised his voice slightly. "May we see some ID, please?"

In full fight-or-flight mode, she stepped away from them, unable to tell her legs otherwise.

"Ma'am. Come back here."

She couldn't. Her ears began to ring and a sickening dizziness overcame her. She focused on the front door. *I have to get out. Get away.*

She managed to look back once and the officers followed her. They were three steps behind her. Frantically, she reached out for the front door just as Brenna came into view on the other side.

Brenna practically caught Sinclair in her arms. She looked terrified.

"Sinclair! What's wrong?" Then she saw the officers. "What's going on?"

"Who are you?" one of them said.

"I'm Brenna Wright, the owner. What the hell is happening?" She put her arm around Sinclair and was startled that she shook so badly.

"Do you know this woman?" The tall officer gestured toward Sinclair.

"Yes, I do."

By then, Lucy had come to the front, holding a cup of coffee. "What's wrong?"

"That's what I'm trying to find out."

"We were following a possible shoplifter."

Brenna pushed past Lucy and the officers, taking Sinclair to the front desk. "What the hell were you chasing her for, then?"

"She wasn't talking to us and she began to leave the scene so we—"

"Officers, there was no scene to leave." It alarmed her how frightened Sinclair had become. She was still shaking and her face had gone pale.

"She came in here and this woman fits the description."

Lucy crooked a thumb over her shoulder. "A woman just walked to the back of the gallery. She has blond hair, too."

The police officers glanced toward where she was pointing.

Brenna held her hand up. "Lucy, show them, please."

After they left, she sat Sinclair down in Lucy's chair and knelt down in front of her. "Are you okay?"

Sinclair nodded but still seemed terrified. "I'm fine."

"What happened?"

"They just…startled me." She stood and waved off Brenna's attempt to hold her. "I'm fine, really."

"My God, I didn't know what was going on. I saw all of you charging out the door and thought the place was on fire."

Sinclair nodded again like someone would respond when trying to comfort themselves with a repetitive motion.

"Would you like something? Some water?"

"Yes."

Brenna looked in her eyes, trying to read them, but saw only a blank stare. "Please sit down. I'll be right back."

Brenna hurried to her office, her mind racing to make sense of the sudden and upsetting occurrence. Was there more to the confrontation than Sinclair and the police were divulging?

She opened her private refrigerator and pulled out a bottle of Voss.

Her first instinct had been to punch the officers in the face because it seemed like Sinclair was running from them. What the hell did they do to her? She was glad she hadn't thrown any punches, but seeing the heart-crushing look on Sinclair's face made her realize she could have. Easily.

She just needed to calm her down and then talk to her. She'd take her straight home and she could unwind from whatever had happened.

When Brenna returned to the front desk with the bottle of water, the seat was empty. Sinclair wasn't standing by the desk either. Brenna stepped into the side gallery room but only Carl and Nina were there.

She stopped and turned in a full circle, sweeping across the gallery. "Where's Sinclair?"

Carl raised his eyebrows. "She...just left?"

Brenna's anxiety rose instantly. "Is that a question?"

"I thought you knew she was leaving."

"No, I didn't. Which way did she go?"

Carl pointed south.

"Like I said, the artists you like," Nina said, bringing up the same topic she had when Brenna was at her place, "are beautiful, mysterious, and need lots of attention."

Brenna could only glare at her before running out of the gallery.

Outside, Brenna raced around to the back of the building. Her parking spot was empty. Sinclair was gone.

CHAPTER EIGHTEEN

Low tide wasn't due until 1:45 in the afternoon, but Sinclair had been out on the rocks since four a.m. In the darkness of the first hour and a half, she sat on a flat spot about forty feet from her staircase, hoping to erase the thoughts that had pursued her while she lay in bed the night before.

The sound of the waves and movement from the far-off lights of a lobster trawler helped dull her brain, but nothing could obliterate the ache that permeated her body.

The sun rose slowly; minutes and hours passed in protracted units that measured nothing but the pain her decisions had caused.

At least she was back in her secure world. She had been foolish to think that her life could ever be more than it was. Taking such an impulsive risk had almost cost her everything.

She was worse off now than when she made the decades-old commitment to stay close to Pemaquid Point. Venturing from her sanctuary had been imprudent and unwise. She had followed her heart, wishing she could be like everyone else: free to travel, free to experience life, free to love.

At once, the cruel reality that she couldn't do any of those things slapped her in the face and threatened to upend her already dismal state of mind.

To some degree, it was too late now, but it was up to her to control whatever safety she had left.

Damn it. You're a stupid idiot.

What she had painstakingly built over the last twenty years was as much as she could ever have. She had done it. She had put herself here. And no one, or no love, would be strong enough to help her.

❖

"What the hell?"

Beanie had come by the gallery the next day after getting a call from Brenna. "That's five times I've counted you repeating that sentence."

"But I just don't get it."

"And that's the fourth time for that one," Beanie said as they sat in the break room in back. Carl, Lucy and the rest of the staff worked on the upcoming exhibition but moved slowly about, noticeably bewildered by Sinclair's sudden departure and Brenna's darkly growing aggravation.

"As soon as I realized she was gone, I grabbed my cell phone and remembered that I can't call her. Damn it, why doesn't she have a cell or even a land line?" She doubted that calling Donna at the Seaside Stop with a plea to get a message to Sinclair would result in much either. Donna seemed to be a bit protective of her. "She keeps pushing me away and I keep chasing her. She's like the runaway artist. She just took off. No talking, no warning."

"Something must have upset her or pissed her off."

"That's just it, Beanie. I have no idea what did it. I was there. I mean, I stepped out for a few minutes, but I'd been there the rest of the time." She gripped her mug of coffee, a potion that normally soothed her; however she couldn't feel anything but confusion and agitation. "Beanie, I really like her. Things were going so well. I mean, she had been quiet a few times, like she had something on her mind or was a little overwhelmed by being in the city, but I really thought she was enjoying her time with me. And then she disappears."

"Well, she's either playing a serious game of hard to get or something's truly bothering her."

"She's too genuine to play hard to get."

"But genuine assumes that she's being real and authentic."

"She is. At least with what I know about her." Brenna lifted her hand. "She's an enigma that I can reach out and touch," she closed her fist, "but can't quite grasp."

"This one's not an easy one, Brenna. I agree that she's not doing this to mess with you. But if you care for her, you need to find out what's going on."

"With anyone else, I'd have given up the first time we argued about going to New York."

"So why didn't you?"

"I want that exhibition. I've already chased her once before. The time this has already taken away from the gallery is adding up, but I really believe it'll be worth it."

"Come on, sis. Is that the whole reason?"

Brenna shook her head in frustration. "I like her." Hitting the counter with her fist, she added, "What the hell?"

Beanie pointed a finger in the air. "And that would be number six."

"Okay, here's a new sentence. Why?"

"That's a new sentence. But that's also the question. And you're not going to get any answers sitting here repeating yourself."

Sinclair walked into the Seaside Stop at nine a.m. Two fishermen, who were leaving with Styrofoam cups of coffee, held the door open for her, nodding as she entered. The place was void of bar patrons, and Donna, who unhurriedly wiped the back counter, had her back to the door.

"Have any strong coffee?"

Before she turned around, Donna said, "Depends on the depth of the problem." She faced her and added, "I have whiskey at the ready, too."

Sinclair sat down on a stool. "Maybe I should upgrade to a nice tumbler of cyanide."

"That bad?"

"Worse."

"Well, Mr. and Mrs. Bellamy aren't due until game time, and if anyone else comes in, I'll shoo them away." She poured two shots of whiskey, pulled over a stool that was behind the bar, and sat down. "What's the matter, honey?"

Sinclair told Donna about her whirlwind feelings for Brenna and the trip to New York. She talked about how much she loved Brenna's family and how wonderful being with her made her feel. She described the comfort of being in her arms and how time had flown by in the city.

"It all sounds good so far," Donna said as she followed the whiskey with two cups of steaming java.

"Something happened and I ran. It had nothing to do with Brenna, well, not directly. I got spooked and took off."

"What did it have to do with?"

"Me. I didn't feel safe all of a sudden. It's hard to talk about."

Donna patted Sinclair's hand. "I understand that parts of your life and certain feelings are off-limits. We haven't known each other all these years for me not to respect that. So just tell me what you can."

Sinclair searched for the right words. "There's a wall that I don't want and wish it wasn't there, but it is. On one side of the wall is me, the real me, and on the other side is Brenna and the rest of the world." She gazed into her coffee, shaking the cup until little mahogany ripples bounced against one another. "I know if she saw what was on my side of the wall, she'd run."

"I don't understand."

"She doesn't know who I really am, Donna. Not really. You're closer to me than anyone else, and even you don't really know me."

"I know you're a beautiful woman, and I'm talking about your soul, too. You haven't told me exactly what happened to you, but I imagine it was pretty bad. It kept you and me from ever getting really close when we were together. And, honey, I can tell that it's happening again, and this monster of a wall is ruining your chance with Brenna."

"I want to protect her from all this, Donna. I can't be in her life but I can't get her out of my heart. All I do is think about her."

"Why can't she be in your life?"

"Because it'll only go bad." She held her head. The headache she'd spent the night skirting was flaring up significantly. "Haven't you been listening to me? This can't happen."

"How long are you going to keep running? Huh? Till you die an old lady that someone finds washed up on the rocks? Everyone's got a secret, Sinclair. Everyone's ashamed of something."

Donna swiveled on her stool and grabbed a bottle of whiskey and a shot glass. Then she pulled out a bottle of aspirin from under the bar. She filled the glass and plunked two pills next to it.

As Sinclair downed the aspirin, Donna said, "You're going to have to weigh the possibility of true love against what happened in your past and ask what's more important. The easy answer was the one you gave our relationship, but it wasn't the right one."

The more she said, the more scared Sinclair became.

"Don't make the same mistake."

The soldering iron stopped working. Sinclair had five pieces left to place in the window but no heat with which to melt the lead solder to the iron cross pieces.

She had to keep going. She clicked the iron on and off.

Her thoughts about Brenna would return if she couldn't keep working on the goddamn window.

She pulled the plug out of the wall, checked it, and reinserted it.

Come on, you fucking piece of shit.

As she tapped the iron against the palm of her hand, it remained cold.

She grabbed the iron handle with both hands and raised it over her head. With a yell of anguish, she brought it down hard on the edge of the table.

Fuck-ing-piece-of-shit.

She threw it to the floor, where it landed with a crash, and yanked the cord out of the wall. Swinging the back door open, she stepped out onto the deck and grabbed the railing.

She messed everything up. She'd fallen in love with Brenna when she had no right to. Her anger flared deep inside and she shook the railing as hard as she could. The wood cracked but she didn't care. She'd tear the fucking place down.

A white blur came from above, spiraling down about sixty feet in front of her. She stopped shaking the railing and looked out toward the rocks. It looked like a seagull, but whatever it was now lay on a large rock, flapping in distress.

She ran down the steps and swiftly navigated her way over the rocks and toward the bird. As she got close, she slowed down to reduce any anxiety about her presence. The seagull wasn't flailing so much now, but its chest puffed rapidly and his eyes were fixed in a stare.

Sinclair knelt close and noticed its side was badly gashed and bloody. It wasn't a gunshot wound because a large portion of his wing had been half torn off, not blown off.

She looked out over the water. A seal had probably attacked the bird. It must have pulled away right as the seal had taken a ferocious bite, and this was as far as it had gotten. She couldn't help the seagull, who was breathing more slowly now.

"Poor thing," she said quietly, and sat down cross-legged.

The bird stopped fluttering, then began to shake slightly. Finally the seagull stopped moving altogether.

Tears flooded her eyes, washing together the white color of the seagull's body with the charcoal of the rocks until the whole image was as obliterated as the poor bird.

"I'm sorry," she cried. "I'm so sorry."

She began to wail in despair for the bird, for Brenna, for her heart, and for her entire life.

Chapter Nineteen

Brenna pulled into Sinclair's gravel driveway just before ten o'clock that night. The house looked dark but Sinclair's car was there.

She walked over to the side door. The small incandescent bulb overhead glowed dimly, looking the same as it had, not long ago, when Sinclair greeted her at 5:35. That morning, Sinclair had a smile that could move even the darkest of clouds from anyone's heart.

Off to the right, along the foundation of the house, lay a hump of dirt. It looked like a newly dug grave for a small animal. A tiny cross made of driftwood stood at the base. A piece of green sea glass on a copper wire hung from the cross.

Brenna leaned over the porch railing to look in the side window. Only a lone light in the kitchen was on. She knocked on the door.

She had spent the last hour rehearsing the things she would say when she saw Sinclair. She'd prepared questions about what happened and statements about her feelings for her. But beyond a few opening bits of dialogue, she didn't know how the conversation would go. She ran through the gamut of possible causes for Sinclair's departure, from something she said to something she did. But over the miles of highway between New York and Maine, she'd come up with dead ends every time. Why had Sinclair left?

She was compelled to make the drive and, though it was taking too excruciatingly long to get to her, it was the best way to find out what had happened. She missed Sinclair terribly. And whatever had caused such terror in her eyes had broken Brenna's heart.

She knocked again but Sinclair didn't answer.

Maybe she was out. If so, Brenna intended to stay there until she got back. She decided to walk around to the back porch and wait.

In the dark, a lone figure sat on the deck. Brenna's heart leapt and she stepped up onto the porch. "Sinclair?"

Sinclair turned to look at her but it was too dark to make out any expression.

"What are you doing here?"

"I…I…" She stuttered in response to the intimidating sound of Sinclair's voice. "I came here to see you. To talk about what happened in New York."

During an uneasy silence, Brenna shifted her weight, and the wooden creaking sound conveyed her nervousness.

"Let's just say it's not going to work."

"What do you mean?"

"There's not going to be an exhibition."

Brenna's voice suddenly exploded from her. "I don't care about the exhibition!" And in a moment of surprise, she realized that was true.

"No, Brenna. *We're* not going to work."

Brenna took a step forward. "Sinclair, what do you mean? I thought things were going well between us."

"The distance. Your life, my life."

Despite the dark, Brenna could tell she was shaking her head.

She took the last few steps to reach her, but Sinclair stood and backed away.

"Sinclair, I'm confused. I don't understand what's going on. Take me inside so I can see you."

Sinclair opened the back door and stepped in. She turned on a light and walked over to her work table. Propping herself against it, she crossed her arms. "We can't be together."

Bewildered, Brenna said, "Is there someone else? Is that what it is?"

"No. There's no one else. I never would have been with you if there was."

"I didn't think so, but I've been trying to figure out what happened between us."

"Please, I need you to respect my feelings and leave it at that."

"What feelings are we talking about, exactly? The emotions we shared in New York, making amazing love, and enjoying the hell out of each other? Or am I supposed to accept this new declaration that isn't a feeling at all, but some command that I'm supposed to salute and then march right back to New York?"

"I didn't ask for this, okay?" Sinclair's voice shuddered as she yelled. She took in a breath and her voice calmed. "Look, I shouldn't have…I…can't be with you. I'm sorry I left so abruptly. I know it confused you. But I need it to be this way."

"This way meaning us not being together?"

"Yes."

"Sinclair, I really don't understand any of it."

"Just understand that I've decided that I can't be with you, okay?"

Brenna snapped her fingers, frustration building. "Just like that?"

"Go, please."

"Why? What did I do?"

She raised her hands to her forehead, rubbing it rather roughly. "You didn't do anything."

Brenna began to say something but Sinclair interrupted her. "It was my fault that anything ever started between us. I never should have done that to you. It wasn't fair and I'm sorry."

"You can't help your heart," Brenna said. "And I can't help mine."

"That's just it, I could have. I should have."

"Do you really believe that?"

"It doesn't matter what I believe." Sinclair squeezed her forehead with one hand.

"It does to me."

"Don't do this, Brenna."

"I drove nonstop to see you after you just disappeared. I deserve an explanation."

"I didn't ask you to come up here."

"Then what am I supposed to do? Just leave and forget we ever met?"

Sinclair's head ached terribly, but the pain in her heart threatened to make her physically sick. "Yes."

"You're trying to push me away."

"I'm trying to correct a mistake."

"You and I were a mistake?"

Sinclair hated her stepfather and brother with a dark, boiling anger that almost ruined her, and until now, she'd never felt the same way about herself, but her next words would change that forever.

"Yes. An absolute mistake." She couldn't look at Brenna, choosing to stare at the floor instead. "Leave now. Please."

The silence proved almost too much. Sinclair fought with every ounce inside her to remain stalwart. And with each voiceless second, her heart bled that much more.

When she heard footsteps moving away from her and then the miserable sound of the closing door, she shut her eyes to catch the tears that came.

❖

"Sis, what's the matter?"

Just the sound of Beanie's voice helped fill the wretched emptiness that had spread through Brenna since she left Sinclair's. She had driven only a couple of miles before she was crying so hard the dark road blurred in front of her. She pulled over and broke down in a frenzy of sobbing that came so fast she thought she'd never stop. Eventually, her body couldn't maintain so much distress and she quieted. She let her head sink until she felt the cool leather of her steering wheel. Outside her car window, the forlorn rustling of the trees kept her company, but otherwise she felt utterly lost and alone.

A cold silence grew in the car, and the longer she stayed there, the worse she felt. She wanted to leave but she couldn't think clearly enough to navigate the dark back roads that led to the highway. She picked up her cell phone. Thank God Beanie was home.

"It's about Sinclair."

"Is she all right?"

"I drove up here to find out what happened. I saw her but I didn't find out much."

"She didn't tell you anything?"

"No. But she did say it's over between us."

"What? I can't believe that."

She sniffled. "Neither can I, but she means it."

"What did she say exactly?"

"That it won't work and she can't be with me. She said she's sorry she left so abruptly, but she needed it to be that way."

"Is there someone else?"

"No. And I believe her."

"I don't get it."

"I don't either. I never expected this. Not with the way things were going between us. It was perfect." She wiped her eyes. "She's amazing and loving and made me feel like no one has ever been able to."

"Oh, sis, I'm so sorry."

"Have you ever felt physical pain over someone?"

"Of course. Like you're going to die."

This was a new concept to Brenna. "I never have before."

"The more you want something, the more it hurts when you lose it."

"I could have sworn she wanted me as much as I did her. I could feel it, you know?"

"You'll bounce back. It'll be okay."

Her heart didn't feel like it would be okay. Her sister had told her the same thing most times when she broke up with someone, and each time she agreed. But this time was vastly different.

"That's just it. I've always been all right. Until tonight. Things in my life have come with little effort, including the women I've dated. But was that because of the relationships I chose? I know now that they were easy and uncomplicated to begin with."

"Yes, it was obvious you could take or leave most of the women you dated. At least the ones I met."

"You pretty much met them all."

"And I like Sinclair the best by far."

"But it's over," she said as a jolt of anguish shot through her. "God, this hurts."

"Something's bothering me, though."

"What?"

"She told you she can't be with you. Saying you *can't* isn't the same as saying you don't want to."

Her comment made sense, especially since Sinclair wouldn't look at her at the end. When she'd told her she made a mistake, Sinclair just kept her head down.

She looked out through the rain-dotted windshield. Branches blew their unwanted leaves onto her hood. "I'm not coming home right away."

"What do you plan to do?"

"Find out what she means by *can't*."

"It's late, sis. Find a hotel and get some rest. You're pretty wrung out right now and I imagine Sinclair is, too. Talk to her in the morning."

Her sister was right. Brenna was exhausted. It was close to midnight so she prayed that the Pine Cottages had a room.

"I love you, Beanie."

"Love you, too."

CHAPTER TWENTY

I think you've had enough."

Donna was frowning. She didn't understand. If she did, she wouldn't be holding back the booze.

"I've only had four shots."

"And you rarely drink more than one or two."

Midnight had come and gone, and a few tired fishermen warmed up with bourbon or Irish whiskey after a cold day on the ocean. Shortly after Brenna left, Sinclair had gone to see Donna at the Seaside Stop. She couldn't remain in the house and hear the echoes of the cruel words she'd spoken to her.

True, she needed to end it with Brenna, but the last thing she'd said had been a lie. Actually, a half lie.

Being with Brenna wasn't a mistake, at least not for Sinclair. It was the best thing that had ever happened, her chance at the truest, most sublime love of her life.

But it wouldn't be the same for Brenna. If Sinclair allowed the relationship to continue, Brenna would unquestionably see the mistake.

Sinclair had had to decide for her.

"Another shot of whiskey, please."

"I'll pour you one more if you tell me why."

"Because I want one."

"No. Why do you want one?"

"Brenna came to see me tonight. She wanted to know why I left New York, but I couldn't tell her everything. Besides, the details don't matter. We can't be together and that's what I told her."

Donna poured another shot into Sinclair's glass.

"The look in her eyes. Donna, it crushed me. But she doesn't understand."

Donna leaned forward on the bar. "Honey, no one understands. You keep your life so clandestine and tight against your chest. People who meet you want to know who you are. It sounds like you and Brenna really found something special, so of course she's going to wonder why you broke it off."

Sinclair tilted back the shot glass and the whiskey burned unsympathetically as it went down. "I didn't expect her to come all the way up here."

"If I hadn't lived just down the way when you and I split, I would have driven across the country to try to change your mind. But you're stubborn, and while that makes you a strong person, it can also make you very lonely."

"I hurt her."

"It sounds like you did. And since you're drinking my liquor, I'm gonna tell you something. If you're determined to keep your life secret you shouldn't have started a love affair with Brenna in the first place. It wasn't fair to her. You can't get involved with someone and then just leave them cold."

"I don't know what I was thinking. She was mind-blowing, Donna. My heart fell right into her."

"And I'm sure hers fell right into you."

Sinclair felt woozy. The whiskey was definitely doing its work. But she was still miserable. She'd wanted the alcohol to numb the memory of Brenna's face when she'd told her to leave. She wanted to erase the expression of pain and confusion she'd caused.

"Another shot, please."

"So this is how it's going to be?"

Sinclair focused on the bottle of whiskey, just out of reach.

"You play the recluse until someone interesting comes along and you step out of your shell, and it feels good, but all you can do is run back home and slam the door."

Sinclair closed her eyes, willing Donna to stop talking. Her brain became a dizzying, alcohol-drenched whirlpool. Somewhere outside her head, Donna's words sounded like the buzzing drone of insects. She opened her eyes to gain her equilibrium.

"Fishermen come in here after losing a buddy to the sea. Men who have spent forty or fifty years devoted to a woman who's just died come in here. I let them forget their sorrows because they've earned it. You haven't. Here you are thinking that you have the right to drown your life in a bottle of booze. But the person that deserves the most is Brenna. She deserves an answer."

Donna picked up the bottle of whiskey and moved it to the opposite end of the bar, setting it down with a loud, liquidy clunk.

❖

Brenna woke early to the sound of a semitruck rumbling by, booming and shaking the window of her room at the Pine Cottage. She lay in bed debating whether to drive out to see Sinclair again. She'd already been dumped so why should she subject herself to more rejection? Still, she couldn't shake the feeling that Sinclair didn't truly want to be without her. She felt agitated and nervous. Was it worth the trouble to pursue a woman who had told her it was over? Worse, one who had said their relationship was an absolute mistake?

With anyone else she'd been with, those words would have made her immediately shrug and turn on her heel. Easy. Done.

Sinclair lived hundreds of miles away and could be difficult and ornery. She was secretive and enigmatic. She'd challenged her when Brenna had simply gone to her house to talk to her.

Pursuing Sinclair was a foreign quest. Of the women who had broken up with her, she couldn't remember a single one she'd been tempted to chase.

Her past relationships had been too much work, and too much work meant her feelings never grew as deep as they maybe should have been or needed to be. She'd never grown roots but rather remained a transient in the world of love, free to make whatever decision served her.

Unlike her gallery, where she never gave up on her pursuits, relationships were too difficult. Why would she spend any time chasing something that was a gamble or might take focus off her business and prove disastrous?

Then she compared the two compartmentalized parts of her life. At the gallery she chased risky art and artists all the time. There was always a possibility that a deal she made could turn disastrous, but her "never give up" mantra kept her focused and determined. As long as she followed her credo, she made it through the treacherous and shaky situations. The end result was always worth the effort. If she gave up easily on acquisitions, she'd never have the success that she enjoyed.

She could follow her gut on upcoming trends and artistic innovation. She was free to charge through adversity and obtain whatever she coveted. Her energy and fortitude were limitless.

But in her love life, she operated quite the contrary. She ran from relationships when the slightest sign of difficulty reared its head. As soon as an obstacle popped up, she would run.

And where had that led her? To her very own, self-created, prison of loneliness.

She threw her hands over her eyes. She was a fugitive of her own devices.

But Sinclair had also floored her with intense emotions and desire. And Brenna hadn't even thought twice about driving to Maine to see her, not the first time and not the second time, especially since her feelings had grown immeasurably in between.

She'd run from every woman she'd ever gotten close to. And now, she'd run from the one woman who had ignited feelings inside that far out-burned those she'd had for anyone else.

Petra was another life ago, it seemed. Sinclair wasn't Petra. And her gallery didn't give her the excitement, and pleasure, and tenderness that Sinclair did.

CHAPTER TWENTY-ONE

Sinclair awoke in the back room of the bar. Donna was gone. She remembered talking with her until she closed the Seaside Stop and Donna ushered her into the back, pushing her down on the couch in her office.

Sinclair got up and checked for a hangover. Other than some cobwebs in her head and a rather dry mouth, she felt tolerable.

The bar stood empty but she called out for Donna anyway. When no one answered, she went behind the counter and poured herself a club soda. With a flick of her wrist, she saw that her watch read five thirty. Donna would be coming in soon to open up, but Sinclair didn't want to be around when she did.

She'd already had her butt chewed out, which she deserved, but she didn't need to listen to any more. She just wanted to limp home and crawl under the covers for a few hours.

After she put the glass in the sink she patted her pockets for her keys. They weren't there.

Looking around, she finally spotted the bowl at the end of the bar. A sign reading Keys Here, Then Drinks was taped to it. She plucked her keys out. Good thing, she thought. There are a lot of trees between here and home.

Stepping outside, Sinclair allowed the darkened morning to soothe her mood. She inhaled, hoping the crisp air would refresh her unsettled mind. Looking out onto the main road, she expected Donna to pull up any minute. She scanned the road and then something across the street caught her attention. Brenna's car was parked in front of one of the rooms at the Pine Cottages.

Shit, why couldn't she be gone already?

Her heart immediately ached. She wanted to start to forget Brenna this very morning. She wanted to drive home and fill her time with beachcombing and artwork. She prayed to return to a lifestyle that existed of her once-a-week trips into town for groceries, a stop in to say hi to Donna, and then an escape back to the only place where time seemed to freeze.

She had to put Brenna and New York behind her, except, there she was. Right across the street.

God, she wanted to see her. Nothing had made sense since she'd run from New York. She yearned to be stricken with amnesia, but Brenna pervaded every brain cell. She couldn't complete a thought or reach down to pick up a piece of sea glass without an intoxicating wave of memories engulfing her. When she stopped for a moment and closed her eyes, she still felt Brenna's sensual hands and soft lips. The recent hours and days had passed as slowly as a decrepit old man shuffling across a wide thoroughfare.

She was nothing more than a reclusive deserter of love, rebuking its romantic promise. She had spent her life in a constant fight to be invisible, but Brenna had seen her. And Sinclair had let her in.

Going backward seemed intolerable now. If she went to Brenna, she risked uncovering a truth that could ruin both of them. If she got in her car and left, she would return to her self-imposed exile. The former could end badly but the latter would be just as disastrous.

She stared at Brenna's motel door. She had to at least apologize for what she'd said.

❖

Great, Brenna thought, I'm up again at the crack of dawn without a cup of coffee in sight. After a fitful night of sporadic sleep and troubling dreams, she'd dressed but now fell back onto the bed in complete confusion about her next move.

If only she could call room service and have them bring up a pot of steaming-hot, highly caffeinated coffee. That seemed like the only decision that would produce positive and predictable results.

A knock on the door made her sit up.

Great. She'd yearned so badly for java that she was now imagining a man in black pants and white shirt standing outside with a linen-covered table ready to be wheeled in. Maybe she needed more sleep.

The knock came again.

She frowned at the early hour and crept toward the door, opening it slowly.

"Sinclair." She looked troubled but was still as beautiful as ever. Brenna stepped aside and let her in.

"May I sit down?"

Brenna pointed to the bed. "Sure."

She sat down next to Sinclair and waited for her to speak.

"I'm sorry I was mean to you last night. I said some things that were partially true, but you must have taken them to heart. When I said I was trying to correct a mistake, I meant that I had made a mistake in believing that I would be okay stepping out of my own little world here.

"I've carved out a life that's safe and has few ripples. It's stayed the same way for twenty years. But then I met you and everything turned upside down. I fell hard for you and let things progress when I shouldn't have, which led to my hurting you." She inhaled deeply. "Brenna, hurting you was the mistake I made."

Brenna still wasn't clear about what had happened. "I hear what you're saying, but the generalizations about you and us don't make sense."

Sinclair rubbed her hands on her thighs, her growing agitation pervading the room like an uneasy wind that precedes a storm.

"When you just up and left New York," Brenna said, "I was concerned. And when I came to see you last night, I admit, what you said devastated me. Sinclair, I need to know why you left."

For the longest time, Sinclair surveyed the room as if searching for something that would help her. "I needed to get out of there."

"My gallery?"

"New York."

"But why?"

"Brenna, please. I came here to apologize and to let you know that you're a beautiful, loving woman, but I just can't be with you."

More vague, sweeping statements. "I don't get it."

"My life isn't conducive to a relationship."

"That was far from true in the short time we were together in New York."

"I loved being with you, I really did. But it couldn't last. I didn't want our final conversation to be the one we had last night, so please accept my apology and let's just leave it at that, okay?"

Brenna's frustration escalated. She wasn't going to let Sinclair throw her away that easily. "That's not good enough."

Sinclair gave her a defiant, challenging look, but a heart-crushing vulnerability lurked behind her expression. "I can't let this go on."

"You're not making any sense. One minute I'm having the best time ever, and I'm sure you were, too. And then you took off. Did Nina's comments offend you?"

Sinclair shook her head.

"Was it those police officers?"

When she didn't respond, Brenna said, "Please tell me."

Obviously Sinclair was having a silent argument with herself. She looked at the floor, her eyes darting around.

Brenna reached out to take her hand but Sinclair raised her shoulders as if she was cringing, and Brenna withdrew her hand.

"Please. Just tell me the truth."

Sinclair gazed straight at her, her eyes filled with tears. "The truth. The truth will make you turn away from me…or turn on me."

Brenna wanted to hold her, to make whatever was tormenting her so badly just disappear. "You're already trying to get me to turn away, and I'm not going anywhere. I'm crazy about you, Sinclair."

Sinclair closed her eyes, shutting them tight, as if to expunge some horrible thing, and Brenna's mind raced trying to figure out what it could be.

"Whatever you have to say will be okay."

For a long time, she stared past Brenna, her eyes red and filling with tears. Brenna saw sadness, tinged with something else. Fear? Shame?

Then Sinclair focused on her, looking deeply into her eyes. "I murdered my stepfather."

CHAPTER TWENTY-TWO

There you have it. That's the truth." Sinclair clasped her hands together, but they were shaking.

The words had staggered Brenna, and the ragged gasp of breath she took was the only sound in the room.

Sinclair stared hard at her, as if steeling herself for a bad reaction. After a moment, she said, "I always thought that if I ever told anyone, they'd be disgusted and repulsed, not hurt."

Brenna opened her mouth but didn't know what to say. In a moment, the admission had come like a wrecking ball slamming into an old wooden shack, and her world had exploded. Brenna's overworked impulse to run was strong. Her head buzzed and her throat went dry.

"Brenna, I don't go anywhere because if they find me, I'll go to prison. Do you understand that?"

"Yes." Brenna's voice came out barely above a whisper.

"After I killed him, I ran. That's how I ended up here twenty years ago. I'm sure they looked for me—the police, my stepbrother—but no one knew where I went. I hitchhiked, walked, then hitchhiked some more. I don't remember much except for hiding along the roadside at night, sleeping in culverts or behind gas stations. And then I ended up here. Peggy found me and took me in. She fed me and clothed me. She was the only one who knew what happened. No one else does, except you, now."

Her body sagged with the weight of the horrible secret she'd held for two decades.

"I've been hiding ever since."

"When the police confronted you in New York," Brenna said carefully, "they scared you."

"They asked for my identification. With computers and fingerprinting software and other technical stuff nowadays, I was sure they'd figure out who I was."

"I'm so sorry, Sinclair."

"No need to be. I did it. I've gotten it in my head that one day someone will find out who I really am, and I'll have to pay the price." She paused and then stood. "That's why we can't be together."

She stepped toward the door and Brenna said quickly, "Wait—"

"For what? Nothing's going to change where we are right now. You know the truth and you know why I left New York." She smiled weakly, or maybe it was a grimace. "We can't be together, Brenna. I wish we could."

After she walked out the door and closed it carefully, Brenna stared at it for a long, agonizing time.

❖

Brenna sat on the motel bed until seven thirty. She seemed to have gone into a trance, her brain churning relentlessly until she became numb and frozen in a sickening, dreamlike stupor.

The sounds of people talking outside and cars and more trucks driving down the highway rumbled at the edge of her consciousness until another thunderous semi finally roused her. In a daze, she collected her things and picked up her car keys.

She couldn't think of anything to do but return home.

❖

It's over. The words followed Brenna down the highway and past Damariscotta and Wiscasset. She joined Interstate 1 South and watched dully as the blacktop road, with its aged cracks and patches, stretched out before her like an endless quandary.

Needing gas, she finally pulled off in Falmouth and filled up. With little energy and no desire to get back on the road, she detoured to Foreside Harbor and got out of the car.

The boatyard, for its small size, was dynamic with the comings and goings of skippers and their vessels. Normally this type of environment would energize her. She knew that picturesque places such as this were where her clients would find inspiration for their work. Maybe all that was left was to make the long drive back home and bury herself in the gallery again. She meandered around, willing the sea air and moderate breezes to ease the discord in her gut and eventually found a tired-looking floating dock that sat deserted and isolated from the busy fishing commerce not far away.

Sitting on the warm wood planks, she leaned back and ran her fingers across the uneven texture of the worn boards. A lone seagull scrutinized the stability of a buoy not far out in the water. The bird landed and jostled for balance a moment before tucking its wings and settling in to bask in the same patch of morning sun that warmed Brenna.

Memories of Sinclair, their lovemaking and walking around New York, muddled together with imagined scenarios of Sinclair at fifteen being abused and beaten and finally retaliating against her father. Her heart ached and sharp, physical pain gripped her chest. She thought of Sinclair's escape and being alone out on the highway, scared and hungry and trying to survive.

She'd lived her life as a prisoner, hiding from prosecution for the intolerable circumstances she was subjected to.

A fugitive, Brenna thought, fleeing from something extremely tough.

Brenna had fled only from relationships. And they hadn't been tough, or complicated, or even abusive. So why was she always walking away?

Too much work. Not enough emotional investment.

Since Petra, she'd moved through every relationship the same way on an easy, unimpeded path, doing, or not doing, as she wished, whichever was easier.

What had been the outcome of that behavior? She was nothing but a quitter. Here she was again, leaving a relationship that wasn't easy. Too much of a struggle.

The conversation she'd had with Sinclair at Rockefeller Center came back with stinging clarity.

She had told Sinclair she'd never struggled for anything. She had been right, she wasn't a strong person.

She now knew her biggest character flaw. After hearing Sinclair's shocking revelation, Brenna had grabbed her car keys and driven away. She'd pushed her feelings for Sinclair aside because they hadn't fit into her game plan. She'd fled like a pathetic deserter.

She'd caused her own misery, and sudden shame washed over her because Sinclair's troubles were a thousand times worse than hers.

Oh, Sinclair. The one woman who finally meant something to her and the one that made her feel breathlessly alive and enormously happy. She had every reason to stay away from such a catastrophic disclosure and the ramifications that could follow, but every time Sinclair would look at her, Brenna would melt into those emerald eyes. They contained such a powerful expression of trust and vulnerability that was all for her.

Could it be love?

She looked out at the crisp, blue water, understanding the weight of her realization. No matter how difficult Sinclair could be, Brenna could no longer run away from her heart. The woman she'd fallen in love with now compelled her to take the most important stand of her life.

No, it's not over.

Before she said it aloud, she nodded slowly, a familiar chant now ringing true in a previously closed part of her life.

"Never give up." She stood so quickly the seagull launched itself from the buoy with an annoyed cackle.

CHAPTER TWENTY-THREE

B renna still hadn't found a cup of coffee all morning, but getting a fix was far from important. With the noon hour upon her, she drove back into New Harbor and straight to Sinclair's house.

She banged on the door, waited anxiously, and banged again. Her nerves were on edge and some caffeine would really help, but nothing was more important than what she was about to do.

Sinclair opened the door. She looked like she'd been crying.

Brenna stepped closer. "I can't shut my feelings off like that."

Sinclair turned and walked toward the windows facing the sea. "Neither can I. But it doesn't matter, Brenna."

Brenna followed her, stopping right behind her. She could almost smell her blond hair. "Of course it matters."

"Think about a relationship where one person is in hiding. I won't let all this drag you down. It was foolish to think you and I could be together and not have any problems."

"That happened a long time ago."

"By law, there's no statute of limitations on what I did, Brenna. They can come get me any time. What kind of a life could we have? What kind of a lover could I be if I'm always worried about being arrested? What kind of healthy relationship could come from what I've done?"

"You're not the same person now. You're incredibly loving and considerate. You're kind and passionate—"

She whirled around to face her. "I'm a murderer, Brenna."

"And a thousand things other than that."

"You're not getting this, are you?"

"What I get is that we have feelings for each other. Am I wrong about that?"

"No."

"Well, then, listen to me, now. When I drove away from town this morning, I was numb. I didn't know how to react to what you said. But then I started to think about us. And I thought a lot about me and how I've been in relationships. I've always left them so easily because I never really, truly cared about the women I was involved with. I know some were more important to me than others, but they never meant all that much.

"With you it's not that easy. Now that I've met you, everything's different. I don't want to give up. I came back because I realized I've always wanted to have this relationship. I can't imagine walking away without ever knowing what we could be like together.

"I'll help you, no matter what. I don't know what that means exactly, but I'm ready for whatever happens."

For the longest time, Sinclair stared out to sea. Brenna could tell she was listening but wasn't sure if what she said had made an impact on her.

Sinclair's confession had shocked her. She had figured Sinclair must have been harboring some kind of secret, but she never imagined something so serious. However, the only facts that ran through her mind while she sat on the dock in Falmouth were the ones that had to do with the Sinclair she knew right now, the woman she so very much wanted.

If she had continued to New York, she would have been, yet again, bailing out on a relationship. But this time, no matter what consequences the past events might bring, she had decided to go with her heart.

Sinclair raised her head and took Brenna's hand. She led her over to the work table and they sat.

"I might as well tell you everything. The night I…the night it happened, there had been fights all day. That wasn't unusual, but that day seemed to be really bad. My stepfather had already had a fistfight with my stepbrother, who then came into my room and pounded on me. He would take his anger out on me because he knew I couldn't fight back as hard as our father.

"I told you before that my stepfather was a dairy farmer in Waterville, New York. Well, after my stepmother died, things really got bad at home. He drowned his problems in booze and finally lost the farm. When I was twelve, we moved about thirty miles away to Little Creek. I thought having next-door neighbors so near would keep my stepfather and brother from the abuse, but it got worse.

"Anyway, the night it happened, I stayed in my room as much as I could and tried to block out their yelling. I was fifteen and couldn't wait to be sixteen so I could get a driver's license and a job, and leave.

"I eventually needed to go to the kitchen to make dinner." A sad chuckle came. "It was buttered noodles." She shook her head. "Anyway, the three of us sat at the table while I listened to them scream at each other in an extension of the fight that had been going on all day.

"As soon as I cleaned the dinner dishes, my stepfather started drinking in the family room, and my stepbrother came and got me and we drank out on the front porch.

"I was learning that alcohol helped me forget my problems. As much as I hated my family when they drank, I understood why they were doing it. I'd never had more than a beer up to that night, but I kept drinking. When we ran out of booze, my stepbrother went back inside and stole another bottle.

"A lot of that night is just patches of quick memories. He and I talked about how much we hated my stepfather. I remember saying I wished he was dead."

She paused. "I don't know how long we were there. Anyway, at some point I wasn't feeling well and tried to get up from the chair to go to the bathroom.

"I wish I could remember more. Sometime later, I ended up shooting him where he lay passed out on the couch. I remember my stepbrother freaked out, telling me I needed to leave because I'd go to prison for the rest of my life. I was so sick, and all I wanted to do was go to bed. I think he helped me pack some things, I don't know. He might have said something like he wouldn't call the police until I was gone."

Brenna listened to the nightmare of a story. It shocked her, but what rendered her speechless was the weight of keeping such a secret and the horrible memories that must still relentlessly haunt Sinclair. The heaviness of her expression broke Brenna's heart.

All of a sudden, it seemed the weight of Sinclair's confession fell squarely on her shoulders, because she bent over and caught her head in her hands.

Brenna moved closer and wrapped her arms around her. She started to shake then poured out the hard, wracking tears of so many bottled-up years. Brenna let her cry, giving her supportive squeezes and moving the wet tendrils of hair from her face.

Much later, after Sinclair had quieted and rested her head on Brenna's shoulder, Brenna coaxed her to the bedroom and helped her into bed.

As Brenna stood over her and pulled up the covers, Sinclair took her hand, tugging it gently.

She climbed in next to her and Sinclair fell asleep in her arms.

Chapter Twenty-four

Sinclair awoke alone to music playing lightly in the front room. She listened to what must be the local radio station, because a Phil Collins song ended and she recognized the voice of the DJ. Her eyes felt puffy and sore, and when she sat up, her head thumped mercilessly. It was late afternoon and it took her a moment to get her bearings.

It's out, she realized. She had spilled everything to Brenna that morning, and now the sharp sting of remorse cut through her. But what surprised her was the mix of feelings that jumbled up inside her.

She was petrified now that someone knew her secret. After twenty years of guarding the truth, she had confessed it, and the sour bubbling in her gut was the fear of no longer having complete control.

But she also felt extreme grief over her confession. It brought back many deliberately suppressed memories of the man who had adopted her, fed her, and raised her. However, the beatings she'd suffered far outweighed any fatherly recollections.

Strangely, her stepfather wasn't the complete source of her anguish.

After fleeing Brenna and New York, she had driven the first hundred miles or so in absolute fear. She felt brain-dead from the sudden onslaught of what she'd perceived as a threat. She'd barely thought about anything more than hands-on-the-wheel and drive-the-speed-limit. Not until she'd reached Hartford, Connecticut, did she begin to process what had happened.

A simple case of mistaken identity on the part of the police officers had made it evident how easy it would be to get caught. She had no business being in New York, which meant she also had no business being in a relationship with someone who lived there.

By the time she'd crossed into Maine, she knew she had been foolish to believe she could be in a relationship with Brenna. One stupid, fucking decision when she was fifteen had formed the rest of her life, and she wouldn't subject Brenna to the mess she had created.

Brenna didn't deserve to be with a killer. And as chickenshit as it sounded, Sinclair didn't want to spend the rest of her life in prison.

When she'd arrived home, she dove back into her cocoon, back where she belonged, with no more false hopes or stupid notions. It had been ridiculous to masquerade as a normal person who could fancy having an out-of-town lover.

She had freed Brenna from further problems and now things would return to the way they had to be.

But then Brenna had come after her, and the only way she could get her to stay away was to tell her the truth. Though Brenna had said she would help her, no matter what, she'd never be able to handle a disaster this big.

Like a student afraid to face the principal, she forced herself to get off the bed and face the reality of her past.

Brenna sat at the table with a cup of coffee. She looked so beautiful in the waning afternoon light that remorse stabbed Sinclair.

"Hi," she said softly.

"How do you feel?"

"Like I have a hangover." She sat at the table and Brenna fetched a cup of coffee for her.

Brenna sat back down with Sinclair's drink. "This will help."

"Thanks for staying, although I'm not sure why you did."

"How can you say that?"

"Brenna, it's not like I confessed to stealing bubble gum from a dime store. I killed my stepfather and took off. And now I've condemned myself to a secluded life here. That's the choice I made. The only other one is going to prison." She felt sick and spoke her next words as gently as she could. "Either way, there's no way this, you and I, can work."

"It can, Sinclair, if I know one thing."

"What?"

"How do you feel about me?"

Sinclair smiled faintly. "Meeting you made me understand what love really feels like. Being in your arms is so powerful. An energy that's almost too intense to understand makes me want to jump up and run and yell that I'm head over heels."

"That's what love's all about."

"And that's what makes this so fucking hard."

"Don't renounce us. Don't deny what you feel."

"Don't you see that I have to? My life is ruined because of something I did. Yours doesn't have to be."

"Sinclair, I know we hardly know each other, but the connection I feel with you astounds me. I knew my ex-girlfriends much longer but liked them so much less." She held up an open hand in emphasis. "I want to be with you."

"Please, Brenna. Throw in the towel before it gets worse."

"Never give up."

"What?"

"Never give up. It's something I believe in, Sinclair."

"Maybe this time you shouldn't."

Sinclair looked out toward a lobster boat bobbing in the waves. Brenna's heart thumped against her chest as she watched her.

When Sinclair turned back, her eyes seemed sadder than before. "You say you've never struggled for anything. I've struggled all my life. I endured my stepfather's beatings and wiped up my own blood. I got good at lying about my scars and the burn marks from his cigarettes. When my stepbrother got old enough to smoke, he put out his butts on me, too. I was destroyed by the time I was ten, and by the time I left, I was used to the sick routine. And it made me into someone that isn't...normal."

Brenna leaned forward, the determination inside her hammering. "You entrusted me with your secret, knowing that the truth could drive me away. And you must be feeling very fragile right now." She picked up a cobalt piece of sea glass and held it up. "This got broken and beaten against the ocean's rocks, just like you did years ago. And you're as exposed as this glass is right now. But look at it. Maybe it's not the same as it used to be, but it's stronger than ever. And more beautiful.

"When you told me what happened, I was shocked. What stunned me weren't your actions, but the weight you must have felt from keeping such a secret. I can't imagine all the horrors of the abuse, but the heaviness in your eyes, and the way the pain physically pulled your face down, cut right through me.

"I won't leave you now. Not when you cared enough to confide in me. I don't know what will happen, but I can imagine how horrible it would be if I walked away from you without knowing what could be."

Sinclair's head dropped and she began to cry. Brenna moved closer and wrapped an arm around her shoulder.

"I was programmed to believe that I didn't deserve mercy or love. I know it was all bullshit, but that stupid record keeps playing in my head."

"Let's begin to erase it."

"I want to think that I can. I look at you and feel absolute trust, and that terrifies me," Sinclair said as her head slowly came up. "If I can't believe in you, I might as well give up completely. But I don't want to give you up." Fresh tears ran freely down the folds on either side of her nose. "I'm so tired of running and hiding."

Brenna began to open her mouth but Sinclair said quickly, "I know. Never give up." She wiped the last of her tears with the back of her hand. She looked away and surveyed her belongings.

The long silence stretched out, with the rumble of two sets of waves marking the duration. Finally, Sinclair said, "There's only one way to truly stop running."

As if taking an inventory of all the things that made her feel safe, she finally said, "I need to go to the police and face this."

Brenna took her hand. "I love you, Sinclair."

"I love you, too. And I'm scared to death."

Chapter Twenty-five

Things began to move quickly for Sinclair. After years of staying put, she was about to leave her safe cocoon again, but this time the world would know who she really was. However, an odd sense of relief tempered the waves of fright that constantly washed over her. At times, she felt a glimmer of hope and promise, but it was too fragile to trust.

Brenna went back to New York, but only to arrange for a longer absence from the gallery. She would return in three days and accompany Sinclair to Little Creek, New York, where she would turn herself in and answer for her childhood decisions.

She hadn't thought much about Little Creek in recent years. She wanted to forget the old neighborhood with its small houses that were close enough to the railroad tracks to feel the rumble of the trains that came through.

Those were the same tracks she had used to get out of town. The first night, she'd walked and run alongside them until it was so dark she could no longer make out exactly where the gravel on the side of the tracks met the grass. She didn't want to trip and sprain an ankle so she'd pushed her way into some bushes to sleep.

The next morning she found a road and followed it, until the pain in her empty stomach forced her to stop in a roadside café.

When her stepbrother had told her to get out of town, she'd had the presence of mind to take the money she'd been saving for a new CD player.

The pancakes on the café menu looked so good. She counted the dollars and change she'd hastily stuffed in her pocket. She had just over forty dollars. How could she justify spending one tenth of that on pancakes when she didn't know where or when she'd ever get any more money? Sinclair's stomach painfully rumbled again so she ordered a small side of hash browns instead.

Sinclair put some soothing music on to try to push the dark cloud of anxiety out of the room. Her body felt heavy and even making a cup of tea was so arduous, she had to sit down on her couch. All the arrangements she had to make before she left Pemaquid Point swirled around her mind and daunted her. Should she turn off the utilities and board up the house against nor'easters? It depended on how long it would be before she came back. Then again, would she ever return?

Sinclair lifted the teacup to her mouth but was too nervous to drink.

She thought about Petey, the squirrel. She would have to leave a huge pile of nuts for him because she might not…

The tears came so fast they flooded her eyes and spilled onto her cheeks before she could even gasp at the finality of her life.

She still had time to change her mind. Only one person knew the truth. But if she did, she'd be back where she started, alone and constantly looking over her shoulder.

She put the teacup down and stood. Her legs felt as heavy as the waterlogged timber that washed up on shore, and it occurred to her that the gloomy fog that had moved in over the coast perfectly matched her mood.

Her neck and shoulders ached as she gazed out over the water. She'd reached a point in her life where having true love was possible. However, if she started a new uncertain life, it would completely destroy the one she'd created. She couldn't have both.

It was truly all or nothing, a crazy gamble where, either way, the outcome didn't favor her. The tide could recede all the way back to Europe and still wouldn't be as low as she felt at this moment.

Had her confession been the biggest mistake of her life?

She turned toward the kitchen and put away some dishes. She adjusted the towels that hung on the handle of her stove. She prayed these mundane things might ground her and provide a sense of normalcy.

This house, she thought, my little place of solace and refuge.

But now, the comfort she sought had evaporated like the morning's sea mist on her windows. As long as she'd lived alone in the house, she'd never felt lonelier. She longed for Brenna, who would hold her and tell her she would be okay. Because right now, she didn't feel like she would.

CHAPTER TWENTY-SIX

B eanie's jaw had dropped and her mouth hung open, but she hadn't yet said anything.

"I'm letting you know about Sinclair and where we're going, but I don't want you to tell Mom and Dad," Brenna said.

She sat in her flat with her sister. The sun had descended behind the city skyline, and lights were coming on in the apartments and lofts beyond her large windows.

"I can't believe—"

"It was a long time ago, Beanie. Sinclair was fifteen and had been badly abused all her life."

"I know. I meant I can't believe she survived."

"She's decided to turn herself in."

"What will happen to her? To your relationship?"

"I don't know. But we want to be together."

"I suppose the future looks a little dicey now, huh?"

Brenna nodded. "I'm afraid we may lose our chance at a life together before it can begin."

"You know how Mom is with your girlfriends. No one's good enough for you and with this…"

"I could be with Princess Kate and Mom would still think it a threat to my gallery."

"Petra did mess you up, you know. You stayed locked up with her in that little love nest for so long, the delinquency notices were piling up at the door."

"That was a long time ago, too. My business is important to me and I know that. But I also know I can't keep taking my cues from Mom."

"Are you scared?"

"Which one, of a thousand things, are you referring to?"

"Sinclair. You know…what happened to her father. That she… did that?"

"No." Her heart ached for Sinclair. "If I'd seen him beat her, I might have done the same thing."

"Really?" Beanie looked frightened.

"I don't know. I mean, I have the power that comes with being an adult now. I would call the police and make sure he never touched her again. She was so young, and maybe she didn't think she had any options."

"Aren't you worried she'll go to prison?"

"I am. Very much so. That's what's so scary about this whole thing. But I won't walk away from her now."

"I suppose you have to gamble. You can't live together on the lam."

Brenna chuckled weakly. "No, we can't. Listen, I've met with a defense attorney my lawyer recommended and told her about Sinclair. She said she'll meet us in Little Creek."

"When are you leaving?"

"Tomorrow. I'll drive back to Pemaquid Point and pick her up."

"Be careful, sis."

"I'll be fine," Brenna said. "It's Sinclair I'm worried about."

Long stretches of silence punctuated their drive along Interstate 90. Brenna drove while Sinclair gazed out the passenger-side window.

"I haven't been on this road in a long time," she finally said.

"What do you remember?"

"Hitchhiking with some really nice people. I stayed out of cars that didn't have another woman in them and did all right. Some gave me a few dollars, which really helped."

"Was it scary?"

"At night, yes. Most of the time I found a covered, out-of-the-way place, and no one ever bothered me. The cold, rainy weather was the worst part, especially since I didn't have any extra clothes."

She continued to look out the window. "When we moved to Little Creek, my stepfather couldn't farm any more because he couldn't afford any land so he did manual labor at the hydroelectric plant. He began to drink a lot more and it got worse."

"The abuse."

Sinclair nodded.

"I had a little radio in my room, and I'd listen to a classic rock station, especially Elton John and Jackson Browne. I had to keep the volume low because my stepfather only liked country. Any little thing could set him off so I tried to remain invisible and just listen to my music."

Raindrops dotted the windshield and Brenna turned on the wipers.

"We don't really know each other," Sinclair said. "Not well, I mean."

It was a surprising non sequitur but Brenna just nodded. "You know me well enough to let me come with you."

Sinclair seemed to contemplate Brenna's statement. "I don't know what's going to happen, but I'm glad you're here."

"It'll be okay." Brenna took Sinclair's hand.

Sinclair looked back out the window.

❖

They checked into a motor lodge in Little Creek, right off the highway. It was late and the sun had already gone down. Brenna couldn't see much of the town. What would it look like in the morning when the sun came up?

Would it be a sleepy little place? Would it look quaint? Or faced with a scary and unknown outcome for Sinclair, would it appear sinister?

"I know I've asked you more times than I should, but are you doing all right?"

Sinclair sat on the bed. "Now that we're here, I'm more tired than I thought I'd be."

"Emotionally tired?"

"Probably." She ran a hand through her hair. "There's so much I don't remember about that night. I guess I blocked a lot of it out. But now that we're here, I wish I could recall more."

"You've been through a lot already. And the drive couldn't have been relaxing. How about we get something to eat?"

"Do you mind if we stay in? I don't want to go out."

"I can pick up something."

"I'm not hungry."

Brenna joined her on the bed and put her arm around her. "Then let's just rest. We don't have anything to do until we meet the lawyer tomorrow afternoon when she gets in from New York."

"What's her name?"

"Marie Alvarez."

"Is she nice?"

"She's nice to clients and mean to adversaries."

"That's good." She looked around the room and repeated slowly, "That's good."

Sinclair's small talk touched Brenna deeply. It was so unlike her. She wanted to protect Sinclair and comfort her, but she looked so lost she wasn't sure what to do.

"Tell me what you need, Sinclair."

It seemed like she didn't intend to answer, but she eventually said, "I want to go back and see the house. See if my stepbrother Topher is still there."

"Are you sure?"

"Maybe he can help me remember things."

"Okay." Brenna caressed Sinclair's hair. "Tell me what you need right now."

Dark circles underlined Sinclair's eyes. "Just be here."

Brenna wrapped her other arm around Sinclair and held her tight. She could do that.

CHAPTER TWENTY-SEVEN

T he window shutters of the house were unhinged, and white paint, yellowed from age, peeled from them like wilted petals off a dying flower. The roof seemed to sag from years of neglect, and trash and old newspapers covered the front porch. The night-jasmine bushes, which Sinclair remembered smelling fragrant and sweet, had become brown clumps of lifeless stubble.

Brenna slowed the car to a crawl and stopped at the front curb. Sinclair gripped Brenna's thigh, appreciating the comforting hand that covered hers.

The dwelling that provided a stage for the atrocities that robbed her of her childhood appeared to have fallen victim to the same abuse.

The neighboring houses hadn't been kept up much better; however, they felt alive with plants and toys and bicycles in the yard.

"There's a truck in the driveway," Sinclair said.

Brenna turned the ignition off. "Do you think it's your stepbrother's?"

"There's one way to find out."

Sinclair grew more anxious with each step she took up the broken cement walkway. Details of the house she had erased from her mind now brought back sharp, cutting memories.

The metal mailbox still loosely hung beside the front door. Her stepfather had slammed her head against it the day she locked herself out of the house and he had to get off the couch to let her in. The second window on the left still had cardboard in it instead of glass. He had punched it out, shattering it in a fit of rage when she served dinner late, then repeatedly hit her, his cut hands spraying blood everywhere.

She felt a hand on her back and realized she'd stopped walking. The horrible memories assailed her like gale winds heralding a storm.

Her feet wouldn't move as echoes of old yells, screams, and crying reverberated in her ears.

"Are you okay?"

"Dad, don't! I'm sorry! Don't!"

The kitchen drywall cracked with the weight of her body being slammed against it. Glass broke from beer bottles thrown close to her head. Doors crashed closed, and framed pictures smashed into countless shards.

"Sinclair, are you okay?"

A bird warbled nearby. A car rumbled by on the street behind her.

The echoes of violence stopped.

She opened her hands and stretched her painfully tight fists. The tension left her shoulders as she willed them to relax and drop.

She began to answer but the front door flew open.

"What the hell are you doing here?"

Topher was so much taller than she thought he would be, his straight blond hair just as unkempt as she remembered. And his salutation hadn't changed.

Everything was both surreal and familiar.

She glanced down at his hands, callused and scarred, with dark grease or oil imbedded in the lines and wrinkles of his skin. Those hands had hit her many times. Like smaller versions of her stepfather's at the time, they could also deliver painful blows.

"I said, what the hell are you doing here?"

She shuddered once, then looked him directly in the eyes. "I'm going to talk to the police."

"What the hell for? You got away with it."

"It's never left me, Topher."

"You think it's never left you? I still live in the same damn house you killed him in."

She hadn't expected a happy reunion, but hadn't they at least been children surviving a nightmare together?

"I just need some answers first."

"I suggest you turn tail and get the hell out of here while you still have your freedom."

"I don't remember a lot and—"

"Do you know what you're doing? You're flirting with prison by showing your face around here."

From behind her, Sinclair heard Brenna say, "Can't you at least just listen to her?"

He leaned toward her so quickly, Sinclair thought he would punch her. "Who the fuck are you?"

Sinclair put her hands up. "Topher, I'm going to turn myself in soon and I just wanted to talk to you for a minute."

He was still staring at Brenna, his eyes angry and threatening.

"Topher…"

"There ain't nothing I can tell you that will help anything."

"How did I get the gun? I can't remember."

"How should I know? It was where it always was, on his nightstand."

"Did you see it happen?"

"I was out on the porch."

A female voice from inside the house called timidly, "Topher, who's that?"

"Keep your nose outta this," he yelled.

Brenna touched Sinclair's arm. "I think we should go."

Topher sucked on his teeth. "There's nothing here for you. Get the hell out of town."

Sinclair stepped backward until she felt Brenna's hand on her shoulder. Topher glared at her like she was a vacuum salesman who had inconveniently interrupted his day, then turned his back on them and slammed the door.

Brenna and Sinclair got back into the car and Brenna started the engine, saying, "Let's go back to the hotel."

Movement in the house next door caught Sinclair's attention. Drapery shifted and someone peered out. As they drove away, Sinclair watched the woman in the window as the woman watched her.

CHAPTER TWENTY-EIGHT

The morning came too quickly. A miserable gray drizzle had settled upon Little Creek, making the day glum and melancholy.

Brenna had awoken with her arm around Sinclair. As she looked out the window, through the moiré pattern that the raindrops made, she pressed closer to Sinclair's warm body. The cadence of her lover's breathing told her she was awake, too.

"Good morning."

Sinclair's hair tickled her cheek. "Good morning."

"Did you sleep?"

"A little."

A gust of wind rattled the window frame as if it were trying to get in. Brenna prayed that the clock would rotate backward, giving them more time before Sinclair turned herself in.

They listened to the rain pick up, tapping more hurriedly against the glass. How miserably fitting, a storm was coming.

Sinclair spoke quietly. "When will the lawyer arrive?"

"Early this afternoon. Probably around one. She wants to meet you here and make a plan. Until then, we could stay here or go out and get something to eat."

"I want to go back."

"To your house?" Brenna feared the toll that another visit with Topher might take on Sinclair. He might call the police, and it wouldn't be good if they came out to get her before Sinclair could turn herself in.

"Not exactly."

"What do you mean?"

"I need to talk to someone else."

Sinclair knocked on the door of the house next to Topher's. Someone shuffled around inside and, eventually, the door opened. A woman about Sinclair's age stared at them. No one spoke for the longest time.

Then the woman said, "Tamara."

Sinclair nodded slowly.

The woman's eyes opened wider and then darted quickly to the left. "There's a café on West Main, just past School Street. Do you remember where that is?"

Sinclair nodded again.

"Meet me there in an hour." The woman closed the door.

Without saying anything else, Sinclair turned and walked to the car. Confused, Brenna followed.

As they got in, Sinclair said, "Drive away." She pointed straight ahead.

"What's going on? Why was she—"

"She's afraid."

"Of Topher?"

Sinclair nodded once more.

Forty-five minutes later, Brenna and Sinclair sat in the car in the parking lot of Bailey's Café. The rain fell heavily now, a protective, watery veil that obliterated much of their view.

Brenna broke the silence that had fallen inside the car. "She called you Tamara. Is that your real name?"

"Yes. I changed it to protect my identity, for one thing."

"And the other?"

Sinclair's jaw tightened. "I grew to hate my name. I used to hear my stepfather yell it when he was looking for me. Most of the time he'd be drunk and call me with this sick, high voice." She seemed to be looking beyond the rainy window, out to the past. "It always sounded like the keening of a crow being slaughtered."

Brenna couldn't imagine what that must feel like. Such an awful childhood, and now Sinclair was suffering all over again by being back in the town she'd run away from so many years ago.

She thought about their very new relationship. She felt more involved with Sinclair than anyone else ever.

With her exes, it always took so little for Brenna to walk toward the door. Any excuse—a small lie, spending too much time on the computer, or constantly being late—would make her decide to break up and move on. She never wanted to dig in and commit to anyone. The slightest negative personality trait or behavior used to make her call it quits, but now Sinclair was about to turn herself in for murder, and Brenna's heart ached at the possibility of losing her for good.

Maybe she'd been looking for reasons to uncouple herself before. But now, while the elephant in the room begged her to flee, she couldn't leave Sinclair's side.

Sinclair shifted in her seat. "When I saw Clara, I had a foggy memory."

"Clara, is she the neighbor?"

"Yes. When I saw her looking out her window yesterday, I got some vague images, but they're too fuzzy to make sense of."

"I so hope Clara can help."

Sinclair turned to her. "So do I."

After another half an hour, Sinclair said, "She's not coming."

She looked so disappointed and exhausted, Brenna wished she could erase this whole nightmare from Sinclair's past. Of course, that meant they would never have met, but Sinclair wouldn't have had to endure the pain and extreme suffering. "I suppose not. But we'll wait as long as you want."

The rain continued to pummel the car in a loud, persistent assault that added to the bleak mood.

Sinclair gazed out through the rain a bit longer before saying, "Let's just go back to the hotel."

Chapter Twenty-nine

At one o'clock, Brenna opened the hotel room door to a dark-skinned, tastefully made-up woman dressed in a plain black suit and black high heels. She carried an umbrella and a small briefcase in one hand and reached out with the other.

"Good to see you, Brenna."

"Thanks for coming." Brenna led her in and introduced her to Sinclair before offering her a seat at a small table by the window.

Sinclair joined her at the table and Brenna settled onto the bed.

Marie Alvarez extracted a legal pad from her case and clicked her pen. "Brenna told me a bit about your situation but I'd like to hear it all from you, Sinclair."

As Sinclair described the night of the murder, Marie took notes in quick scribbles of her pen rather than long sentences. As the story progressed, Sinclair's voice dropped and she appeared defeated and stressed.

When she finished, Marie stopped writing and finally spoke. "As your lawyer, I must say this to you." She emphasized her words by tapping her pen on the pad of paper. "You don't have to turn yourself in. You do have the right to remain silent about this. You are taking a very weighty step in coming forward. Now, if you decide to go through with this, I will tell the police that I'm bringing in a person of interest in a cold case, but they won't know your name. That way, you can back out if you choose."

"I want to do this."

"Very well. When we sit down with the case detective, I'll let you know if you should refrain from divulging certain things. Without meaning to, you may say things that the police could misconstrue, so please be careful and allow me to interrupt if needed."

"Will they put her in jail right away?" Brenna said.

"Probably, because of the severity of the crime."

"And then what?"

Marie addressed Sinclair. "You will appear in front of a judge, hopefully within a day or two. Bail will be set. I'll be there to argue for a bond reduction. I will argue that you turned yourself in, which might help. Is this your first offense?"

"Yes."

"Then I'll state that. Your statement alone is not enough. They will need to find corroborating evidence—fingerprints on the weapon, something like that. You'll appear in front of a judge for a bail arraignment. The case will then likely go to trial. I'll do everything I can to convince the prosecutor that by turning yourself in, you should receive some leniency, but you should still be prepared for at least a lengthy prison sentence if there's evidence."

Sinclair somberly nodded.

"I'd like you to arrange to stay here until we reach some kind of resolution. In other words, if the judge knows you're not going to escape or even leave the area for a while, it will make things much better for you. Are you able to do that?"

"Yes."

"If you're not released on your own recognizance, the next step would be to pay the full bail amount, if it's affordable or the judge orders a surety, which is a cash bond. If it's not and the amount is too high, you could then go through a bail bondsman. There may be other bail restrictions but we won't know until the judge decides."

"Okay," Sinclair said, but Brenna wasn't sure she was taking everything in. She moved from the bed and crouched next to Sinclair, holding her hand.

"Are you sure you want to do this?"

"Yes, I am."

"I know this sounds selfish, but I hate that we've come this far," Brenna said, "just so I can lose you."

"But if I don't do this, you've already lost me. If I stay in Pemaquid Point, I lose you for sure. We couldn't have a life together with me hiding out forever. But if I turn myself in, I might be able to confront this and get past it all."

Hearing the formality of the lawyer's words made a wall of fear suddenly crash down on Brenna. She wanted to tell Sinclair to forget it all and just go back to Pemaquid Point. "If you'd never met me, you wouldn't be sitting here right now. I feel like I've brought you to the lion's mouth."

Sinclair's smile was strained. "I created the lion. You didn't. I wondered if I'd have to do this one day, but I could never come up with a good-enough reason to. Now that I've met you, I have one."

"But it's a catch-22."

They both understood the predicament well, and Brenna was simply hoping beyond hope. Sinclair appeared to understand that perfectly, but her response was braver than Brenna's.

"As slim as it is, it's our only chance."

Sinclair and Brenna followed Marie into the Little Creek Police Department. They were cold and damp from the rain that seemed unwilling to let up. The officer at the front desk told them to wait, which allowed Sinclair to realize that, ironically, she was waiting to award justice to the sadistic stepfather who, while under his roof, had robbed her of any of her own.

Brenna pulled Sinclair aside. She reached into her pants' pocket, drew something out, and put it in Sinclair's hands.

It was warm in her palm. She looked down and recognized the brown piece of sea glass she had given Brenna, out on the beach, the day after they met.

Brenna said, "You're going to feel tumbled about, but remember, you're resilient and you'll come out stronger."

She closed her hand over the glass, feeling the power in that little piece of Brenna and her home.

They were taken to an interview room where they waited a few minutes until a tall, gray-haired man in beige pants and a baby-blue shirt walked in. Other than the fact that a holster hung from his belt, he could have easily been an elderly schoolteacher or a seasoned insurance salesman. Right behind him was a younger man, quite a bit shorter than the first, but much more muscular. He reminded Sinclair of a fireplug.

"I'm Detective Tally." The first man shook the hand of each of them as they gave their names. "This is Detective Owens." He motioned for them to sit at a small table. Marie and Sinclair sat across from the detective while Brenna took a seat in a chair in the corner, to Sinclair's left.

Marie spoke to Detective Tally first. "So you're the cold-case detective?"

"Cold-case detective? We're all cold-case detectives, and hot-case detectives." He nodded toward Detective Owens. "All two of us." He shuffled through some papers in an old manila folder before looking up. "So you're the Grady girl."

"Yes," Sinclair said.

"Before we go any further," Marie said, "I'd like to point out that Miss Grady has come in on her own. She was a young girl then and she had been badly abused when this crime occurred."

"I agree that this is a very old case," he said, "but it's still murder."

"It's her only offense," Marie said with confidence and authority.

"It may be, but it's the highest level of offense." He paged through the notes and handwritten forms, which looked a little yellowed from age. Sinclair looked away from the pictures of the crime scene. Tally closed the folder as if he knew the case all too well. "Why are you turning yourself in after all these years?"

Sinclair looked at Brenna a moment. Her eyes, so full of compassion, calmed her. "I couldn't keep hiding."

"Well, let's go over what happened that night," he said. He informed her of her Miranda rights, and in the next hour, she had told him everything she remembered. Marie only interrupted once, at the beginning, to remind Sinclair she had the right to remain silent.

Detective Tally nodded a few times throughout but let her finish before saying, "I understand."

Marie leaned forward, as if his response appeared dubious. "What do you mean by that?"

"He was a bastard. I'm not saying he should have been killed, but most folks knew what he was doing to his kids. Topher never got over that kind of upbringing. He's been in jail a number of times since. He's a mean one, too."

This piece of news didn't surprise Brenna.

"So what happens now?" Sinclair asked.

"We have your statement, but we'll need corroborating evidence and we'll go through the things we collected back then. And for now, Miss Grady, you'll be arrested and held here until a judge can hear your case. Would you like to add anything else at this point?"

Sinclair looked down as if measuring the weight of her decision. "No."

Brenna hugged her before Sinclair was led away. She choked back tears, but they spilled out anyway, and she struggled to breathe through a throat that was so tight, she thought it would close completely.

Brenna stood outside the interview room with Marie, numb and frightfully uncertain. "What do we do now?"

"We go back to our hotels. We can't do anything more right now. Let me take care of the next step."

"Which is?"

"We wait for the arraignment and try to get bail. I'll fight to get the lowest amount possible. If the judge orders a cash bond, you'll need to come up with the full amount. If not, you can use a bondsman."

"That's it? We wait?"

"For now. I'll call you when I know something."

CHAPTER THIRTY

Two days later, Sinclair stood before a judge in a small courthouse next to the police station. When the bailiff called, "The People vs. Tamara Grady," Brenna's stomach clenched. Sinclair was brought out in handcuffs and wearing a pale-blue jumpsuit.

The judge took a couple of long minutes to review a file, then asked the prosecutor for a few specifics of the case. After that, Marie made some comments and a confusing exchange of paperwork took place.

The judge then asked the prosecutor to make a statement with respect to bail. He advised the court that he'd recommend bail and that the amount be set at $75,000.

Marie then addressed the court while Sinclair remained silent. She reminded the court that Sinclair came forward of her own accord, had no prior trouble, had lived the last twenty years as a model citizen, and had made arrangements to stay in town. She then requested of the court that she be released on her own recognizance.

The judge made a few notes and set a surety bond of $50,000. He added that if she bonded out, she would have to check in once a week with a court officer.

That was it. In less than five minutes, the arraignment was over.

Again, Brenna watched Sinclair being led away. They were only allowed to share a quick look, and Brenna tried her best to appear confident and encouraging. She held her hand to her heart and Sinclair raised her cuffs, matching the gesture with both hands.

Marie joined Brenna at the back of the courtroom. "Now we have to get Sinclair out on bail."

"I'll take care of that."

Marie handed her a piece of paper. "Here's the name of a local bondsman. It'll take a few hours until she's in the system. I'm going back to my hotel to work on my case notes. Call me when she's out, okay?"

Brenna's cell phone rang and she glanced at the caller ID.

Shit. "Mom. Hi."

"I dropped by the gallery and Carl said you were gone. Where are you, Brenna?"

"I'm on vacation."

"With a show about ready to open?"

"The show's fine, mom."

"Are you with Sinclair?"

"Yes." Though she couldn't see her, Brenna knew her mother had that damn look in her eyes.

"This isn't like you. At least not for a long time. And you know what I mean."

"I know what you mean. And it's not like last time."

"Right before a show?"

Her voice ticked up a notch and it rankled Brenna. "Mom, leave it alone. I love her, do you understand?"

"What I understand is that your father and I invested a lot of money in your gallery. Honey, I'm worried."

As fresh as an ocean breeze could lift her hair and cool her face, a thought washed over her. "I'm going to pay you back for the loan, Mom. I should have done that a long time ago."

"You don't have to—"

"I want to. Need to, actually. I have to go, Mom." It was apparent that her mother had more things to say, but Brenna said good-bye and hung up.

Brenna inhaled deeply, the decision clearing her head quite a bit. She left the courtroom and called her bank in New York.

She needed to have a bail bondsman arrange the full bail amount. For that, she had to pay them a ten-percent fee. She told her bank representative to have $5,000 wired to her.

❖

The rain continued to fall as Brenna drove back to Sinclair's old neighborhood. She had some time while the court processed Sinclair's bail paperwork and her bank arranged for the wire transfer. She hated the thought of Sinclair spending even one moment in jail and would go to the bail bondsman that Marie recommended as soon as she could. But she first needed to do something else for Sinclair.

She parked past Topher's place and walked back to the neighbor's house. She shook off the rain as best she could and rang the doorbell.

The same shuffling noises came and stopped just on the other side of the door.

"Who is it?"

Obviously, Clara had become nervous after Sinclair and Brenna's last visit.

"Clara, my name is Brenna Wright. I'm with Sinclair…Tamara Grady. I need to speak with you," Brenna said through the closed door.

There was no response.

"Please."

The door opened and Clara stepped aside, letting Brenna in. She closed the door and led her to a couch in the front room.

Clara seemed to be Sinclair's age, but she moved with the slowness of an aged person. She had makeup on but it was applied in a clumsy way, as if she rarely left the house.

"Clara," Brenna said as they both sat, "I'm Brenna. It's nice to meet you." Nothing about the situation and the dark, rainy day was nice at all, though. "I imagine you're afraid. Of Topher, I mean, and I understand. Tamara is in jail now. She turned herself in for the death of her stepfather, but she really needed to talk to you. I'm not sure what about, but I hope you can help her in some way."

"Tamara and I were childhood friends." Clara paused and offered Brenna water or coffee. Feeling a sense of urgency, Brenna declined.

"It was such a horrible night," Clara said. "I always wished Tamara could move in with me and my family, to get away from hers, but that still wouldn't have been far enough away. And after that night, she was just gone. There was talk around town about her. The police crawled all over the county but never found her. Some thought she'd killed herself. I even heard that someone found her clothes out by a lake just south of town, like she'd jumped in and drowned." Clara wrung her hands and a long, drawn-out "oh" came from her before she continued. "I can't imagine what it was like to be surviving on her own at fifteen. I thought of her so much over the next few years. I ain't never thought she'd died. I figured one day they'd catch her, but that day never came."

"Clara," Brenna said, "Sinclair said that when she saw you through your window the other day, a foggy memory came back to her."

Clara's hands stopped moving.

"That night...did you see her?"

Clara's mouth tensed and then she nervously licked her lips. "Yeah." She flattened both hands on her knees. "I heard the fightin' that day and into the night, which was usual, but that night, it was worse than that. It had got quiet for a while, that was after the sun gone down. Maybe nine o'clock. I went over to see if she was okay."

"And?"

"I looked into her bedroom window. She was in a bad way."

"What does that mean? Was she scared? Hurt?"

"She was drunk. I tried to get her to leave through the window, because if her stepfather saw her that way, he'd kill her. She laid down on the bed. All she wanted to do was go to sleep."

"She said that?"

"No, she just fell asleep. I called her name a whole bunch of times, but she didn't move."

"And then what?"

"I heard more yelling coming from the hallway close to her room so I got scared and left."

Brenna thanked her and got up to leave. She hadn't heard anything that would help.

"Thank you, Clara."

As if apologizing, Clara said, "That evening...was a nightmare."

But Brenna knew the nightmare wasn't over.

She risked looking toward Topher's house as she drove away. Blowing out a nervous breath, she saw that the front door was closed and the window shades were down.

CHAPTER THIRTY-ONE

S mitty's Bail Bonds office handled her case swiftly and flipped through the paperwork as if she were buying an automobile on a used-car lot. They took her deposit and explained that they would go right to the jail and start the process with the officer attending the front desk. They told her, however, that with the time between the police verifying the bond and sifting through the paperwork, then the final bonding-out, the process could take three or four hours. Maybe more.

Brenna took the opportunity to get something to eat at a local diner and then call her sister.

"So now what?" Beanie asked after Brenna had filled her in on what had transpired since they left New York.

"We get Sinclair out and hope for the best."

"But she's going to trial, right?"

"Not yet. The lawyer is walking us through the procedure, which has a lot of steps. Let's just hope something happens between now and then that helps."

"Are you okay, sis?"

"I feel horrible. It's like I helped turn her over to the wolves."

"But you said she decided to do this."

"All because I met her."

"But if you hadn't met her, she wouldn't have had the opportunity to love."

"Well, not love me. But she could have met someone who wouldn't have influenced her to blow her cover."

"You're second-guessing, Bren. There's a reason for all this. All you can do is love her and support her."

"And bake a cake for her in prison."

"Stop that. You don't need to go there. You have to prop her up and get her through this. Love is a powerful thing, you know."

"I'm not sure I do."

"Well, with Sinclair, it's time you stepped up to the relationship plate. You've lived a pretty happy-go-lucky life. You're not going to like me saying this, but you're a consummate dater who runs when things get weird or heavy. Well, you've got both of those things now, but you also have a wonderful woman."

Brenna had to agree. "She isn't like anyone I've ever met."

"Do you really love her?"

"I'm crazy about her."

"It's easy to be crazy about someone. What I'm talking about is the times when the realities of life come."

"We're facing some harsh realities right now."

"And what do you feel?"

"I'm pretty spun up, Beanie. But I can't leave her. It's like I'm in some kind of altered state. Being with other women was okay. As I look back, I suppose at times dating them was mostly something to do. But Sinclair seems real and my whole life changed when we met. I don't think I ever understood self-sacrifice and compromise as much as I do now. But both don't take anything away from me. It's easy with her. I can't explain it any other way. If this whole mess could somehow be cleared up, I'd sweep her off her feet and spend the rest of my life making her happy."

"Then that's what you do. Go with your feelings. Don't overthink them. You do that too much in the rest of your world."

"How did you become so wise?"

Beanie's laugh was warm and full of affection. "These are the same things you talked to me about when I met Pete."

Nevertheless, her sister surprised her. She had grown into a magnificent and mature young woman.

"I love you, sis."

"Me, too, Bren. Now go help her."

Brenna waited for Sinclair in the lobby of the police station. It was interesting to watch the routines of people who were in the business of serving the community. It was also odd for her to think that these people also wrangled criminals and sometimes shot guns. If it weren't for the uniforms, they'd look like workers in an automobile-warranty department or any other workplace.

Four-and-a-half hours after Brenna left the bondsman, Sinclair was released. She rushed up to Brenna and hugged her so hard, she thought they'd tumble over and land on the ground right in front of two officers who were sharing a story about a recent break-in.

They waited until they were in the car to kiss. It was long and incredible and full of passion.

"I missed you so much," Sinclair said. "Thank you for getting me out. I know it was expensive. I don't know how to—"

"Don't say any more about that. We're in this together, okay?"

Sinclair kissed her again, gingerly holding Brenna's cheeks as if she were a butterfly that might flutter away any moment.

Sinclair looked tired. "I need a shower."

"We're heading straight back to the hotel, then."

As they drove, Brenna filled her in on her visit to Clara's house. Sinclair remained silent for a while, taking in what she was saying with a few nods.

"I'm sorry she didn't see much that would help," Brenna said as they turned into the hotel driveway.

"She did."

"Did what?"

"I need to see her."

"You want to talk to Clara?"

"Yes. Being here in Little Creek has made things become a little clearer. Memories are coming back. Most of them don't have anything to do with that night. I mean, I remember details from walking home from school because we drove down my old street. And conversations come back just by getting food at the grocery store."

"What's coming back about Clara?"

"I'm not sure yet. It's right at the edges of my mind. But I need to see her."

"Let's get you showered and then we'll go."

"Now. Please, let's go now."

CHAPTER THIRTY-TWO

Clara showed them to her couch. "It's been a long time," she said.

"It has," Sinclair said. "Brenna told me you two spoke this morning."

Clara nodded but didn't say anything.

"I remember getting drunk and I'm trying to remember more. You said that I laid down on the bed."

"Yeah. I tried to get you to leave through the window. Mr. Grady was pretty mad, yellin' and making noises. I was scared he'd come in and beat the livin' daylights outta you."

"Why didn't I go?"

"You were all messed up, Tamara. You'd spilled soda or booze or somethin' dark all over you and didn't want nothin' to do with nothin'. You just went to sleep."

Sinclair struggled to recall more from that night. "I don't remember that."

"That's what happens when you're drunk."

"I don't remember just falling asleep."

"She doesn't remember," Brenna said directly to Clara, "because she didn't just fall asleep. She passed out."

Clara looked down and nodded. Tears began to run down her cheeks and Sinclair leaned forward.

"What's the matter, Clara? Tell us."

"Like I said before, I heard Topher and Mr. Grady screaming just outside in the hall so I left. I just left you there. I was scared you'd get beaten so badly. You always had a black eye or punched-up face. Always. But this time seemed real bad. But I left you there. And then I was crossing your lawn, just passing the front door, when I heard the gunshot. I thought he'd come in and found you drunk and killed you." Tears ran down her cheeks and she started clasping her hands together.

Brenna sat there silently for a minute. "Wait a minute. You said you were passing their front door...you mean about twenty feet away from the window? Like, in five seconds?"

She nodded again.

"But you said Sinclair was passed out. She couldn't have come to, found a gun, found her stepfather, and pulled the trigger all in the time it took you to walk twenty feet."

Clara began to cry harder. "I couldn't tell anyone. The next morning, when I heard what happened, Topher had already said that Tamara shot him, and all those police scared me to death. Later, I tried to talk to Topher, but he said Tamara did it and I didn't know nothing. He said he'd kill me if I said anything. For the next few weeks, Topher came around and made sure I knew he was there, like he was watching me, so I didn't say nothin'. I hate to admit this, but eventually things returned to normal and I went about my life. I never had the money to leave this house, especially after my daddy ran off and mom drank herself into her grave a few years back."

She looked up and her eyes were wet and red. "I'm so sorry this all happened to you, Tamara. When you showed up here, I was so glad you was alive, but I'm still afraid of Topher. You don't know what he can do."

"I do," Sinclair said solemnly. "He could kill you." She turned to Brenna, her face flushed. "Like he did his father."

"But you turned yourself in. I need to make right of my wrong."

Brenna spoke next. "Clara, you need to take this information to her lawyer and help Tamara. Do you understand?"

"Yeah."

"Marie will do whatever she can to protect you."

"I'm not sure if it'll do any good," she looked at Sinclair, "but you been through enough. And if there's a chance to get Topher taken away, the whole neighborhood'll be better off. It's been too long."

Sinclair placed her hand over Clara's. "It has been too long. For all of us."

As they left Clara's porch, Brenna hurried toward the car. "Let's go before Topher sees us."

Sinclair's head spun and her emotions boiled hot in her throat. She stopped in Clara's driveway, looking at Topher's house.

"What are you doing?" She heard Brenna but she seemed far away.

This shocking information had frozen her in time. Her vision blurred around the edges and she felt miles away from her body. Topher had physically abused her for years, but in one reprehensible moment, he had committed murder and told her she'd done it. He had exploited her psychologically and had cruelly executed a twenty-year sentence upon her. Her abusive childhood was being played out again. But this time, she was in control. "That bastard."

"Let's go, Sinclair. We need to get to Marie."

Sinclair's vision cleared and she walked toward his porch.

"What are you doing?" Brenna's voice strained with anxiety. "What are you doing?"

She caught up with her at the door, pleading, "Sinclair, don't."

Sinclair knocked loudly.

Topher swung the door open.

"You killed him," she said angrily. "Not me, you bastard. You accused me of murder and made me believe I did it. You banished me from everything I ever knew."

"Stop your jawing. You're crazy."

"I've been looking over my shoulder for twenty years, and now I'm going to take back the life you stole from me."

"You ain't got a life. The police will be looking for you when I call them." He walked inside and Sinclair followed him.

He turned and yelled, "Get outta my house."

"You can't tell me what to do any more. I know you killed him."

"Your fingerprints were on the gun. Go ahead, ask the cops." He jabbed a finger toward her face. "You did it."

Sinclair shook her head slowly, seething at the human piece of flesh that was once her stepbrother.

Topher's face grew red and he looked over Sinclair's shoulder. "Who the fuck are you? You her lawyer or somethin'?"

Sinclair realized Brenna had followed her in. "Leave her out of this."

"You gonna go to the cops and lay some bullshit on them? Huh?" Before Sinclair could react, Topher pushed her aside and grabbed Brenna by the arm, throwing her to the ground.

He dropped down quickly and knelt on top of her. Sinclair grabbed a metal chair leaning against the wall in the entryway. Just as he raised his hand to punch Brenna, Sinclair smashed the chair against him. He rolled off her and clutched his head.

Sinclair reached for her hand. "Are you all right?" She helped her up and pushed her toward the open door.

Topher still held his head but turned sideways, looking up at her. "Fuckin' bitches!"

She grabbed the chair again and raised it threateningly over her head.

"Turleen, call the police!"

Sinclair left him on the ground and followed Brenna out the door. She kept the chair with her until they reached the car. As Brenna climbed in, he appeared at the door yelling obscenities. Sinclair chunked the chair on his lawn and got in the car. Without a word, Brenna started the car and they drove off.

CHAPTER THIRTY-THREE

They returned to the hotel and Brenna still shook from the confrontation. She could barely slide her hotel key card through the slot. She'd never seen a real fight before, let alone been involved in one. It rattled her to the core. There were plenty of fights on the streets of New York, but a car window or a television screen always shielded her. Things had gotten out of control at Topher's house and she couldn't calm down.

She was frightened for Sinclair, but she was also frightened for herself.

"Are you okay?" Sinclair asked her when they were safely inside the room.

Brenna wasn't sure and didn't want to admit it. "Are *you* okay?"

"Yes, other than the fact that I stooped to Topher's level and hit him. I never, ever wanted to end up doing that."

"I'm glad you did because he was going to beat me up."

"I wouldn't have let him hurt you. I shouldn't have gotten you into that. I took you into that horrible house and put you in danger." She sat down on the bed. "I'm no better than him."

"That's not true. You were protecting me. Topher and your stepfather didn't do anything but cause pain and fear. You're nothing like either of them."

"I've spent my whole life hiding. And for what? Nothing! I've lived with a lie I was too young to rationalize or argue against."

"You can't blame yourself."

"I do blame myself. And I blame my stepfather and I blame Topher for the miserable life I've had."

"It's not miserable, Sinclair. We met. And that wouldn't have happened if you'd stayed in Little Creek."

"Have you ever heard of damaged goods?" She poked a finger against her chest. "I'm the poster child."

"That's insane."

"I'm probably that, too."

"That's not what I meant. You've carved a life out for yourself in Maine and moved on from your childhood. And I'm crazy about you. Not the girl that left Little Creek, but the woman you are today."

"I still am the girl that left Little Creek. I could have come forward at any time. But I've become too good at hiding in my house and pushing people away. If my stepfather's goal was to fuck with my head forever, he should be congratulated."

"He didn't win, Sinclair. You came back here. You faced your stepbrother."

"And I could still go to prison. It's his word against mine."

"And Clara's. She can prove that—"

"Prove what? She was a fifteen-year-old girl. She didn't *see* anything. There are no guarantees here." Her body was tense, and Brenna had never seen her so frustrated and resigned. "I turned myself in. I said I murdered him."

"But you didn't know what you know now."

It was as if she didn't hear her. "And the prosecutor will have a field day with someone like me. I'm trailer trash to them," she said, and began counting the evidence with her fingers. "I never went to college. My stepfather was a great model of how to raise kids by beating them. And a belt across the back of my legs formed what I know about love and attention."

Brenna stepped to the bed to sit down next to her, but Sinclair stood up quickly and walked to the window.

"You're none of those things. I have felt such love from you, such real and true care from you, and it's a thousand light years removed from anger and violence."

Sinclair didn't respond. The moments when Brenna seemed to lose Sinclair terrified her. She'd become unreachable when they'd first met and Sinclair tried to push her away. It had happened earlier, in Clara's driveway. It frightened her that Sinclair couldn't even hear her. It was starting again now.

With increasing apprehension, Brenna tried again. "You know how to love."

"Love," she said flatly. "I can run. I can hide. I can have sex. But love? I'm not so sure." She turned to face Brenna. "I've never had a long-term relationship. If you haven't noticed, I suck at 'getting out there.' I've become a wretched recluse that won't leave her home."

"You did run and hide. And you may know how to have sex, but you also know how to make love. With me. And I believe you're very capable of a long-term relationship."

"You've got an answer for everything."

Sinclair had completely disappeared. The tucked-away emotions and alarming remoteness sliced into Brenna like the first cuts of a razor.

She wanted to run. This was too heavy, too complicated.

Brenna knew all too clearly that she could shut down too, and her whole body screamed, telling her to defend herself from the pain of exposure and vulnerability.

"I don't have a lot of answers, but I know how I feel about you."

"You can't have feelings for someone you don't even know. Everything was fine a few weeks ago, and then you come galloping into my life and everything turned upside down. How can you say you want to have a long-term relationship with me…after a few weeks?"

"I know enough about you to—"

"I don't even know myself!" Sinclair yelled, and backed away. "I don't know who I am!"

Sinclair's fists were balled up tight and she bent over the dresser, knuckles white against the hickory-stained wood. "For twenty goddamn years, I thought I was a murderer. I hated myself. I knew I didn't deserve a nice life. I almost ran away from Peggy's kindness because of what I'd done. Or thought I did." She turned to look at Brenna, eyes furious and glistening with tears. "But I needed to eat. I loved her, but I couldn't consider her my family either because I was always afraid I'd wake up and find that I'd murdered her, too. That's why I haven't sought out a relationship or a family. I may not have killed my stepfather, but I've lived like I have for so long, I don't think I'll ever erase the belief from my head."

Brenna moved toward her.

Sinclair hunched defensively over the dresser and held her hand up.

"Don't do this, Sinclair," she said desperately. They were both close to imploding and Brenna hung on to a fragment of hope.

She didn't look up. "What? *Don't give up*"?

The words slapped Brenna hard. She should simply get her coat and walk out the door. Her logical brain tugged at her to muster up what pride she had left and go home.

In the silence that followed, a thick, uncomfortable foreboding rose in her chest, like the moment someone feels she's teetering at the edge of a cliff. The air was charged with a disquieting energy that increased with each passing second.

The bedside clock ticked mechanically. The windows rattled slightly from the onslaught of a wind gust.

And then something inside Brenna clicked. "That's right. You're not going to give up."

"Too late."

Brenna got to Sinclair in two steps and seized her arm, turning her away from the dresser. "You're not going to do this. You're not pushing me away." This was a completely foreign action for her. She'd never stepped up and fought for anything. But her feelings for Sinclair took over completely, and she was more afraid of losing her than of the difficulties they faced. "We're going to walk through this mess and see how far we can get. We're going to fight with all the strength we have. There's got to be something to what Clara said. We need to get to Marie and tell her and she'll fight, too. I'm not letting you go, Sinclair. I love you and I'm not turning away."

Brenna put her arms around Sinclair and held her. Sinclair struggled at first, trying to wrench herself free. Brenna held on tight, much like she would do with a panicky child.

Sinclair screamed, "No!" She fought harder but Brenna wouldn't let go.

Slowly Sinclair's tense muscles started to ease. She finally relaxed, almost crumpling to the floor. With one arm holding her up, Brenna stroked Sinclair's hair and listened to the quiet sobs of the woman she realized she would do anything for.

"You said you'd never really had a family," Brenna said with more conviction than she'd ever known, "but you have one now."

CHAPTER THIRTY-FOUR

This is really good, Sinclair. Do you think Clara would repeat this to the police?"

After the confrontation with Topher and their subsequent argument, they'd called Marie to tell her about what Clara remembered. "She's afraid, but I think she will."

"They'll still need evidence to prove Topher killed the father or, at the very least, that Sinclair didn't. Can you get Clara to come to your hotel? I'll be right over. I need to speak with her."

Within a half hour, Sinclair and Brenna returned to Clara's house and brought her back to their room. Marie sat with her at the small table, while Brenna and Sinclair sat on the edge of the bed.

"This is an affidavit," Marie explained to Clara. "It's a formal statement of fact, signed by you, as to what you witnessed the night of the murder. It will serve as evidence in court, if needed. Do you understand that?"

"What do you mean, if needed?"

"It is very important that you appear in person. However, in the event that you can't, this will represent you."

Clara nodded toward the paperwork that Marie had placed in front of her. "This is insurance?"

"It is."

Sinclair understood what Marie was saying, and by the way Clara inhaled deeply, she knew Clara did as well. If something happened to their witness, at least they'd have her statement.

Clara turned toward Sinclair. "I owe it to you."

She spent the next hour drafting the document with Marie.

Sinclair listened to Clara as she retold the details of what she had experienced that night. Clara finished writing the document by hand and signed it, and Sinclair felt a strange mix of anxiety and relief. "What happens now, Clara," Marie said, "is that we go to the police so you can tell them what you told me."

"Do we come along?" Brenna asked.

"No. They won't want any third parties in the room. Especially one that is relying on the testimony. They don't want any possible intimidation from Sinclair, which could sully the statement."

Marie called ahead to Detective Tally and then left with Clara.

"Well," Sinclair said, "I guess there's not a lot to do now."

"There's one thing." Brenna reached for a plastic shopping bag that sat on the dresser. "I got this when I was waiting for you to get bailed out. I just haven't had the chance to give it to you until now."

She handed the bag to Sinclair. In it was a small radio. She looked up at Brenna.

"What you're going to do now," Brenna said as she came over to the bed and sat down next to her, "is tune that to a station that plays some Elton John or Jackson Browne, and you're going to lie here with me and relax."

Sinclair almost cried at the wonderfully thoughtful gesture of love. A sob gripped her and no words came, so she quietly accepted Brenna's open arms and lay down.

A few hours later, Marie called and Brenna put her on speakerphone.

"I submitted Sinclair's recantation of her previous confession. It's officially in the records now. And then the police took Clara's statement, but it's still a completely circumstantial case. I also told the prosecutor about Clara's statement."

"And what did he say?"

"He said, 'Great. Present it at trial.'"

"What does that mean?"

"It doesn't mean anything yet. He's just blowing hot air at me. But he'll move forward with a trial unless we have evidence to support Clara's statement and Sinclair's recantation."

"What happens next?" Sinclair asked.

"Well, to catch you up to today, every felony case goes to a grand jury that decides probable cause. That happened back when the crime occurred. The detectives shared their evidence and what they knew from interviews, and then the grand jury returned an indictment and issued a warrant on you. So a formal charge has already been made. With this new information, however, I'm going to argue for the charges to be dropped."

"Will they do that?"

"No. Not right away, at least. When I meet with the prosecutor, we'll exchange information. I'll want to know what they think and vice versa. It will come down to corroborating the statements with the evidence."

"What evidence do they have?"

"They told me they have the handgun, the stepfather's clothing, a shirt of Sinclair's, and blood samples. Sinclair, can you describe the shirt you were wearing?"

Sinclair thought hard. "It was my favorite yellow shirt, the one with the green peace sign on it."

"Good, your recollection will help corroborate the facts. Your shirt also had vomit and blood on it. Do you remember how they got there?"

She looked down, trying to picture that night. Suddenly, she knew where the blood came from. "After the second bottle with Topher, I was trying to get to the bathroom before I went to lay down, but my stepfather grabbed me. He knew I'd been drinking and he hit me in the face." She raised her hand to touch the memory of the pain. "My nose."

"Maybe that was what Clara saw on your shirt," Brenna said.

"At the time, all the police had was an unapprehended suspect so they didn't release funds for forensic testing. It wasn't justified at the time."

"Is it now?"

"Yes, but they haven't done anything with it yet. They haven't told me anything more than what they're holding. I don't know if they found fingerprints on the gun or anything else. I'll ask when I call the prosecutor back because there should be reason enough now to conduct tests," Marie said before blowing out a breath that sounded, over the phone, like wind through a straw. "Now we need to wait and see if it corroborates what you remember. Sinclair, you'll need to go to the lab and get your blood drawn. I'll get that set up for tomorrow."

"What good will that do if you can't test it against the evidence?"

"We have to do all we can do, Brenna," Marie said. "Now, what about the vomit?"

A vague and spotty recollection teased the edges of her brain. "My nose hurt," she began, "and then I…and then I was…"

"Take your time," Brenna said.

"I was sick. I threw up. That's why I changed my shirt when I ran away."

"At what point did you throw up? After you knew your stepfather was dead?"

It took more time to reach the information stored so far back in her mind. "I woke up because Topher was shaking me. It smelled awful. I had puke all over me. He made me get up—"

"From your bed?"

"Yes. And that's when he told me I'd killed him."

"So your stepfather bloodied your nose, you passed out, at some point you threw up, and then Topher woke you and told you about your stepfather?"

The realization came into full focus and it stunned Sinclair. She nodded before remembering Marie was on the phone. "Yes."

"So sometime while you were passed out, your stepfather was killed."

She looked at Brenna, whose eyes were open wide.

"Yes."

"Do you know if you had thrown up before Clara came to your window?"

"No, I hardly remember that part at all."

"I'll ask her. It could be important to the timeline I'm establishing."

Brenna said, "This is good, right? That she was passed out?"

"If we can prove it."

"How do we do that?"

"I'm working on it," Marie answered.

CHAPTER THIRTY-FIVE

Over the next two weeks, Sinclair and Brenna camped out in the hotel room and stayed in touch with Marie. She was in New York, preparing for the first meeting with the prosecutor, where they would exchange information and she would begin her arguments for dismissal of the case.

Sinclair went to a lab for a blood draw to be compared to the sample found on the shirt. She also agreed to the police department's request for her fingerprints since she'd run away before they could be recorded in the system.

Their life revolved around the hotel room and a fifteen-mile-or-so radius around Little Creek. Brenna called her gallery every day, making sales, dictating letters for Lucy to send, and giving Carl creative input. Although Sinclair tried to convince her to go back, Brenna missed the opening of her current show, From the Hand of the Artist. They'd had a heated argument over it. Words of pent-up frustration and anxiety tinged the squabble, but through it all, Brenna wouldn't budge.

Though flashbacks from her ex and the danger she'd put her gallery through came in waves each day that she stayed away from work, she tried to push them away. She would get anxious and aggravated, but kept those particular feelings to herself. The last thing Sinclair needed to know was that Brenna's past was agitating her, so she fought to ignore any similarities that arose. Still, it was totally unlike her to miss an exhibition opening, and it weighed heavily on her mind. But she couldn't just leave Sinclair alone in a hotel room, waiting to discover her fate.

Instead, they ventured out of their room almost every day, driving around the local countryside, poking into antique shops, and picnicking by the river.

Halfway through their time in Little Creek, Brenna noticed that Sinclair had begun to grow quiet and distant. She would lie on the bed, listening to music from the bedside clock-radio, and stare at the ceiling. When she did talk, she rehashed the abuse she'd suffered, and they'd have long conversations about Sinclair working through the despicable lie she'd lived with for so long. Those conversations were truly wonderful because, in small ways, Sinclair began to heal. She became angry with Topher, understanding that she was too young and naïve to recognize his actions as cunning and deceitful.

But the distance still remained. Brenna tried to talk to her about it; however, Sinclair seemed unwilling to connect with her long enough to identify what caused her to become so withdrawn.

At one of their lunches at the river, everything finally boiled over.

"Maybe tomorrow we could try dinner at that steakhouse by the hotel," Brenna said while they were eating sandwiches and watching an egret stalk fish on the opposite bank.

"I'd rather not."

"Isn't it a good place?"

Sinclair shrugged.

"All day, Sinclair, you've uttered sentences of no more than two or three words. Please talk to me."

"Okay, then." Sinclair's face flashed to anger. "It reminds me of family dinners there. Nothing but arguing and threatening. 'Eat your fucking supper and let's go.'"

"Okay. We don't have to go there." She had said the same thing about most places in Little Creek, which was why they ate so many meals out by the river. "We could drive up the highway, to another town that isn't so familiar."

"You don't get it."

"What don't I get?"

"You're making plans, acting like we're in a nice, normal relationship. We're not. This is surreal and awful and unbearable."

"Our relationship?" Brenna's own anxiety about her absence from work bubbled up again, setting her on edge.

"What's going on with my life. It'll never be normal."

"I want to spend whatever time we have together, Sinclair. Okay, so it's not normal, but I love you. Let's just try to make the best of things right now."

"Right now. Right now while a prosecutor's trying to throw me in prison." Sinclair grew more disconnected and angry. "And why is he doing that? Because I came from a fucked-up family. Violence was the only attention I got in my family. We fought instead of making decisions. There was no love, Brenna, just anger and punching."

"But you're not living with that family any more."

Her voice got louder. "I am a product of that family. I was a little ball of goddamn clay that was molded not by gentle shaping but by being smashed. That's still inside me."

"Some of it may be, but I don't believe that's entirely who you are now. Our relationship has been wonderful."

"How was I when we first met? I was aggressive and distrustful. I almost slammed the door in your face. And what about New York? I ran from the first hint of conflict." Her cheeks grew red and she was on the verge of tears. "I am not normal."

"You had reason to be suspicious when I came to your place unannounced. And you had reasons for running from the police in New York."

"Brenna, I tried to push you away back then because I can't possibly have a successful relationship with you. Don't you see that?"

Brenna's angst came to the surface and her words became more biting than she intended. "You've been trying to concede defeat with us every step of the way, Sinclair. What about making love? Does that feel like defeat? Does that feel wrong?"

"No, it's not wrong. But that's not real life." She swung her arm toward the river. "This is real life. What happened here." She began to cry, which increased the frustration that Brenna had seen building since they'd started talking.

"I could be heading to prison. To fucking prison!"

Brenna reached for her hand.

"No." Sinclair tried to pull away but Brenna moved closer and drew her into her arms. Sinclair struggled against her but Brenna squeezed her firmly to her body.

"I'm your lifeline. Hold on to me. Please." But Brenna needed to hold on just as tight.

Chapter Thirty-six

W hen they got back to the hotel room, Sinclair walked straight to the bed and lay down. Although still quiet after their ordeal by the river, she was no longer emotionally disengaged. For a long while, they had listened to the sounds of the birds along the banks and watched an occasional fish break the waterline with a single splash. The wind picked up so they had folded their blanket, gathered their lunch material, and held hands as they made the short trek back to the car.

"Thanks for lunch," Sinclair said, hands crossed under her head as she lay face-up. "And I'm sorry for raising my voice earlier."

"Just feel what you feel." Brenna walked to her and Sinclair released an arm, patting her lap with her hand. Brenna climbed on top of her, straddling her at the waist.

"You sure know how to order a mean turkey sandwich," Sinclair said, reaching up to Brenna's shirt. She sneaked a hand under and placed it flat on her belly.

"Instructing deli personnel is one of my strengths."

"So you think you're strong, huh?"

"At some things."

"Think you can keep me pinned down?"

"Here on the bed?"

"Yeah."

"Sure." Brenna grabbed Sinclair's wrists, holding her down. Sinclair smiled and suddenly bucked her hips. Brenna launched straight up, laughing at the surprise, but managed to hold her captive. Sinclair rotated her pelvis to the right, squirming out from Brenna's left thigh, but Brenna regained her hold by locking her leg tight to Sinclair.

Sinclair smiled again. However, it was a mischievous response, because she quickly bucked again, this time with more strength, and with a quick twist of her hips, she sent Brenna flipping onto the bed beside her.

"Stick with your deli-sandwich moves."

Sinclair moved over Brenna and kissed her ardently.

Like a stack of dry twigs, Brenna's passion ignited. Sinclair's heated fingers traced lines down her stomach and hurriedly pushed her shirt up, bunching it around her neck, and Brenna became wet. Sinclair unsnapped her bra with a flick of her hand and Brenna pushed it onto the floor. As Brenna pulled off her shirt, Sinclair did the same, and she grabbed Sinclair again to kiss her and feel her luscious warm skin against hers.

When Sinclair moved down, kissing her way to Brenna's belt buckle, Brenna arched into her and allowed Sinclair to confiscate her pants with a quick unbuckling and a few skillful tugs. Her underwear came next and Brenna moaned her approval.

"I need you," Sinclair whispered as she went down on her.

The flutter of anticipation in Brenna's stomach fell away to the uncontrollable trembling of heightened desire. Sinclair's mouth took Brenna to an altogether new place of longing, one that hammered in her chest and entirely overwhelmed her.

She needed Sinclair, all of her, to take her completely and fervently. She had longed for such an intimate and thorough connection for many days, and her lover now hungrily offered it to her. Her excitement rose swiftly, and with each stroke of Sinclair's tongue, Brenna willingly gave herself, revealing her favorite spots and movements to Sinclair with a deep moan or encouraging words.

Sinclair's breath came quicker and Brenna felt the bed move as her lover's body rocked with hers. Sinclair was as stimulated as she was and Brenna's pleasure skyrocketed. Sinclair moaned louder and Brenna's body exploded in the most exquisite orgasm she could remember.

Time stopped and the world froze as the waves of her arousal began to subside. She closed her eyes, but tears came anyway, spilling down her cheeks and around her ears.

Sinclair moved back up. "What's wrong, baby?"

Unwilling to open her eyes and end her dream, she said, "Nothing bad. Just a lot of emotions."

She shook from the light-headedness and vulnerability of coming so intensely, and Sinclair tenderly covered her with her body.

"I've run from relationships for so long and now that I'm finally letting go with you, they're all flooding me right now."

"I feel exactly the same way," Sinclair said. "I was so intent on building a brick wall between you and me that I almost lost you."

"No more bricks."

"No more bricks," Sinclair said before kissing her ear lightly. "I love you."

❖

Sinclair must have dozed off because darkness now enveloped the room, which intensified the blinking red light that accompanied the ringing of the cell phone. Brenna awoke and wiggled her way out of Sinclair's arms.

"You're on speakerphone again, Marie," Brenna said. "Go ahead."

"I've been able to review the evidence. Sinclair, Topher's latent fingerprints were on the gun that killed your stepfather."

"That's good news."

After a pause Marie said, "But so are yours."

Sinclair looked at Brenna, devastation and confusion suddenly boiling up inside her.

"I don't get it."

"At the time, they tested him for gun-shot residue and found none. You weren't there to test, so you became the person of interest.

They don't have much more information about the weapon. The fingerprints, hair samples, and other DNA in your home were all yours, your stepfather's, and Topher's, but that doesn't mean much since you all lived in the house."

They heard the shuffling of papers before Marie continued.

"I spoke with Clara, and the mess she said she saw on your shirt was dark, like soda or red wine. Turns out it was blood. The vomit was a light-yellow color."

"Noodles and butter," Sinclair said. "It was noodles and butter."

Marie paused, but when nothing more came from Sinclair, she said, "Since Clara only saw a dark-colored stain, that means the vomit on the shirt wasn't there when she saw you from the window."

"This is all about the timeline you mentioned."

"Yes. We need to wait for the lab results on your blood test. We need the whole story. So hang tight for now and I'll let you know facts as I get them. And if anyone asks you to talk about the case, don't. Call me and I'll handle everything."

CHAPTER THIRTY-SEVEN

Marie called three long, drawn-out days later. "The police reanalyzed the latent fingerprints on the gun. It's true that both Topher's and yours are there. The interesting thing, though, is that yours are on the handle and trigger, and his are on the muzzle."

"But that sounds incriminating."

"Topher could have picked up the gun after the crime. But it doesn't rule out the possibility that Topher may have used the gun, wiped his prints off the handle and trigger, and then held it by the muzzle—"

"To place it in my hand while I was passed out."

"Exactly," Marie said. "He could have worn gloves, which would explain the absence of GSR. But here's the best news. I just got the report from the medical-examiner's office. As you probably know, the science of blood-evidence analysis has advanced dramatically in the last two decades. If this evidence had been tested right after the crime, the results wouldn't be as precise as they are now. Instead of narrowing a sample down to five to fifty percent of the population, it can now be statistically accurate down to one person out of several million or even several billion."

Sinclair appreciated the historical significance of forensics, but her nerves were already frayed past the point of being bearable.

"The blood, Sinclair," Marie said, "is absolutely yours. Your blood-alcohol level was point zero four percent. You weren't legally drunk though I'm sure you were spinning. But that's not the significant finding."

Too anxious to interrupt, she nervously held her breath.

"Barbiturates were detected in the sample."

"I didn't take—"

"You didn't," Marie said, "but Topher did. And you had enough in your system, given your estimated body weight at the time, to render you unconscious for at least an hour or more. Topher had to have slipped you the drug to knock you out. Maybe you weren't getting drunk enough, so he had to find something stronger. You said he left to get another bottle of alcohol, right?"

"Yes."

"He gave you the drug to ensure that you'd pass out so he could kill his father. Then he woke you and made you think you had shot him in a drunken stupor. You changed out of your shirt before you took off, leaving the vomit, thanks to your stepbrother, and the blood evidence, with even more thanks to your stepfather. Clara can testify that she saw you barely conscious, and her timeline between leaving you and hearing the gunshot will corroborate the evidence." She paused before saying, "You couldn't have killed your stepfather. You were unconscious."

Sinclair couldn't believe what she was hearing. Marie seemed to have put together a defense that proved her innocence.

"I have some more notes to write up, but I am officially going to the prosecutor and police tomorrow. I'm driving out in the morning and should arrive in the early afternoon."

"Will they drop the case?"

"I don't know, Sinclair, but we have a good shot."

Chapter Thirty-eight

"Soon," Sinclair said, "we're going to know one way or the other."

She sat on the river's edge, leaning back on her hands, feet straight out. Next to her, Brenna sat cross-legged, drumming her fingers on her knees. She'd asked Brenna to take her there rather than wait in the drab confines of the hotel room. She needed to breathe in fresh air and watch the shimmering water, especially since there was still a chance that her days of doing so were numbered.

"Marie's meeting with the prosecutor is taking forever," Brenna said.

Sinclair checked her watch. "It started thirty minutes ago."

"I can't stand the wait."

Sinclair, however, concentrated on the feeling of each second: the cool grass under her legs, a small rock pushed against the palm of her hand, the tickle of her hair responding to a slight breeze.

She watched Brenna, who fidgeted and stared at the water. The line of her jaw was beautiful, though it persistently clenched, causing the muscle under her ear to ripple. This woman had loved her and made love to her. She'd held firm when Sinclair tried to give up. In so many ways, regardless of the impending outcome, she'd saved her.

A familiar chortle sent Brenna springing to her feet. She dug into her pocket and retrieved the phone. "Yes," she almost yelled. She listened for a moment. "Hang on."

She pushed the speakerphone button. "Go ahead, Marie."

This was the call they were waiting for and Sinclair's heart hammered. In a few seconds, she would know her fate. Adrenaline suddenly surged through her and she held her breath.

"I just came from the prosecutor's office. He's dropping your case, based on the blood evidence and Clara's statement. We went over the timeline and he agrees that you couldn't have killed your stepfather."

Brenna yelped with joy but Sinclair froze, absorbing the entire meaning of the news. While Marie said something about Topher being brought in for questioning, the path she had taken for the last twenty years washed through her mind like a river flood, deluging her with quickly passing images. It was mostly horrible and sad, and had led her to a dismal place full of fear and leeriness. Her art kept her sane, but she had desired so much more for herself—opportunities to travel, to live freely, and to not look over her shoulder.

However, if the events that had robbed her of so much had never transpired, she wouldn't be in the arms of the woman who had changed her life. She looked at Brenna, listening so intently to Marie. Her face shone brightly and her hair had remained slightly tousled from their lovemaking earlier that day. Her breath caught in her throat. This wonderful woman, who believed in her and had fought for her, would be next to her when she started a new chapter in her life.

Sinclair was finally free. Previously, she wouldn't even contemplate the possibility because it came with the pain of impossibility. But now a simple phone call and a few words from Marie had severed her chains.

She didn't quite feel like celebrating, though. Her family had been torn apart. Her cheerless childhood had made her and Topher the products of a cycle of familial violence, molding him into an abuser and driving her into exile.

Topher could have chosen a different path, but then again, maybe he couldn't. He had always been such an angry young man, and the tragic decision he'd made that night so many years ago had cemented his fate. She'd never know if he had planned the murder or if the idea had just sprung like a wire worn thin from chafing. She doubted he'd ever reform, but she wished him some kind of peace.

After a childhood of pain and destruction, happiness sometimes seemed like a long, dark tunnel ride away.

But she was confident the happiness would come. One day the scars would fade and eventually her guard would fall completely.

And then she would be whole.

CHAPTER THIRTY-NINE

Sinclair walked out onto the rocks, feeling the crunch-pop of kelp under her feet as she surveyed the washed-up fisherman's ropes and lobster traps. The wind carried a conversation between a Maine lobster captain and his first mate from a few hundred feet offshore as if they stood nearby.

She closed her eyes for a moment, allowing the morning fog to lightly kiss her face and deposit a salty taste on her lips.

Some seagulls argued over a beached fish and the sun was attempting to punch through the clouds. The familiar rhythm of the waves crashing and the silence in between sounded so welcoming and reassuring, it seemed to help cleanse her soul of the lifelong burden she had left in Little Creek.

It had been a long while since she'd collected her sea glass. She looked around, spotting rich deposits in all her secret spots.

Brenna joined her on the beach. "You've got some catching up to do."

"Looks like I might need a co-collector."

"Looks like you do."

"You've been trained to find sea treasure so you'd be a good candidate."

"I'd like to apply for the job right away."

Though they'd have time to collect all the sea glass, she couldn't help but pluck a beautiful, matchbox-sized piece of lavender and hold it up to the sky. Its rounded shape and calming, dark-lilac color enthralled her.

"This, and the red piece you found when we met, will make the perfect centerpiece for the window you asked me to make for you."

"That day you first took me hunting for sea glass. I remember. And it's beautiful."

"I'm going to call the window Freedom."

Brenna wrapped her arms around Sinclair, who rested back against her, feeling her lover hold her tighter.

"How ironic," she said.

"What's ironic?" Brenna's breath tickled her ear.

"If it hadn't been for my stepfather's last act of abuse, there wouldn't have been any blood to prove my innocence, and I wouldn't have been freed from my own imprisonment."

"It's a fitting irony. And one that I'm sorry you had to endure."

"Speaking of fitting, you and I are doing that pretty well, aren't we?"

"Yes. A million times, yes."

The woman she completely trusted loved her no matter what. Their stay in Little Creek had tested their relationship rather arduously. But, determined, Brenna had struggled and risen above her self-admitted inexperience to finally embrace the emotional tenacity deep inside herself. By believing so completely in their union, she had given Sinclair the strength to overcome her doubts about ever having a successful relationship. And now, they could start the love affair of their lives.

She turned to face Brenna, her love for this amazing woman overwhelming her, and moved a lock of wind-blown hair from her face.

"You never gave up."

"Never."

"And now we can be together."

"Forever."

About the Author

Lisa Girolami has been in the entertainment industry since 1979. She holds a BA in fine art, an MS in psychology, and is a licensed MFT specializing in LGBT clients. Previous jobs included ten years as a production executive in the motion picture industry and another two decades producing and designing theme parks for Disney and Universal Studios. She is now a Director and Senior Producer with Walt Disney Imagineering.

Writing has been a passion for her since she wrote and illustrated her first comic books at the restless age of six. Her imagination usually gets the better of her, and plotting her next novel during boring corporate meetings keeps her from going stir crazy. She currently lives with her partner in Long Beach, California.

Books Available from Bold Strokes Books

Haunting Whispers by VK Powell. Detective Rae Butler faces two challenges: a serial attacker who targets attractive women, and Audrey Everhart, a compelling woman who knows too much about the case and offers too little—professionally and personally. (978-1-60282-593-2)

Wholehearted by Ronica Black. When therapist Madison Clark and attorney Grace Hollings are forced together to help Grace's troubled nephew at Madison's healing ranch, worlds and hearts collide. (978-1-60282-594-9)

Fugitives of Love by Lisa Girolami. Artist Sinclair Grady has an unspeakable secret, but the only chance she has for love with gallery owner Brenna Wright is to reveal the secret and face the potentially devastating consequences. (978-1-60282-595-6)

Derrick Steele: Private Dick The Case of the Hollywood Hustlers by Zavo. Derrick Steele, a hard-drinking, lusty private detective, is being framed for the murder of a hustler in downtown Los Angeles. When his best friend Daniel McAllister joins the investigation, their growing attraction might prove to be more explosive than the case. (978-1-60282-596-3)

Nice Butt: Gay Anal Eroticism by Shane Allison. From toys to teasing, spanking to sporting, some of the best gay erotic scribes celebrate the hottest and most creative in new erotica. (978-1-60282-635-9)

Worth the Risk by Karis Walsh. Investment analyst Jamie Callahan and Grand Prix show jumper Kaitlyn Brown are willing to risk it all in their careers—can they face a greater challenge and take a chance on love? (978-1-60282-587-1)

Bloody Claws by Winter Pennington. In the midst of aiding the police, Preternatural Private Investigator Kassandra Lyall finally finds herself at serious odds with Sheila Morris, the local werewolf pack's Alpha female, when Sheila abuses someone Kassandra has sworn to protect. (978-1-60282-588-8)

Awake Unto Me by Kathleen Knowles. In turn of the century San Francisco, two young women fight for love in a world where women are often invisible and passion is the privilege of the powerful. (978-1-60282-589-5)

Initiation by Desire by MJ Williamz. Jaded Sue and innocent Tulley find forbidden love and passion within the inhibiting confines of a sorority house filled with nosy sisters. (978-1-60282-590-1)

Toughskins by William Masswa. John and Bret are two twenty-something athletes who find that love can begin in the most unlikely of places, including a "mom and pop shop" wrestling league. (978-1-60282-591-8)

me@you.com by K.E. Payne. Is it possible to fall in love with someone you've never met? Imogen Summers thinks so because it's happened to her. (978-1-60282-592-5)

High Impact by Kim Baldwin. Thrill seeker Emery Lawson and Adventure Outfitter Pasha Dunn learn you can never truly appreciate what's important and what you're capable of until faced with a sudden and stark reminder of your own mortality. (978-1-60282-580-2)

Snowbound by Cari Hunter. "The policewoman got shot and she's bleeding everywhere. Get someone here in one hour or I'm going to put her out of her misery." It's an ultimatum that will forever change the lives of police officer Sam Lucas and Dr. Kate Myles. (978-1-60282-581-9)

Rescue Me by Julie Cannon. Tyler Logan reluctantly agrees to pose as the girlfriend of her in-the-closet gay BFF at his company's annual retreat, but she didn't count on falling for Kristin, the boss's wife. (978-1-60282-582-6)

Murder in the Irish Channel by Greg Herren. Chanse MacLeod investigates the disappearance of a female activist fighting the Archdiocese of New Orleans and a powerful real estate syndicate. (978-1-60282-584-0)

Franky Gets Real by Mel Bossa. A four day getaway. Five childhood friends. Five shattering confessions...and a forgotten love unearthed. (978-1-60282-585-7)

Riding the Rails: Locomotive Lust and Carnal Cabooses edited by Jerry Wheeler. Some of the hottest writers of gay erotica spin tales of Riding the Rails. (978-1-60282-586-4)

Sheltering Dunes by Radclyffe. The seventh in the award-winning Provincetown Tales. The pasts, presents, and futures of three women collide in a single moment that will alter all their lives forever. (978-1-60282-573-4)

Holy Rollers by Rob Byrnes. Partners in life and crime, Grant Lambert and Chase LaMarca assemble a team of gay and lesbian criminals to steal millions from a right-wing mega-church, but the gang's plans are complicated by an "ex-gay" conference, the FBI, and a corrupt reverend with his own plans for the cash. (978-1-60282-578-9)

History's Passion: Stories of Sex Before Stonewall edited by Richard Labonté. Four acclaimed erotic authors re-imagine the past...Welcome to the hidden queer history of men loving men not so very long—and centuries—ago. (978-1-60282-576-5)

Lucky Loser by Yolanda Wallace. Top tennis pros Sinjin Smythe and Laure Fortescue reach Wimbledon desperate to claim tennis's crown jewel, but will their feelings for each other get in the way? (978-1-60282-575-8)

Mystery of The Tempest: A Fisher Key Adventure by Sam Cameron. Twin brothers Denny and Steven Anderson love helping people and fighting crime alongside their sheriff dad on sun-drenched Fisher Key, Florida, but Denny doesn't dare tell anyone he's gay, and Steven has secrets of his own to keep. (978-1-60282-579-6)

Better Off Red: Vampire Sorority Sisters Book 1 by Rebekah Weatherspoon. Every sorority has its secrets, and college freshman Ginger Carmichael soon discovers that her pledge is more than a bond of sisterhood—it's a lifelong pact to serve six bloodthirsty demons with a lot more than nutritional needs. (978-1-60282-574-1)

Detours by Jeffrey Ricker. Joel Patterson is heading to Maine for his mother's funeral, and his high school friend Lincoln has invited himself along on the ride—and into Joel's bed—but when the ghost of Joel's mother joins the trip, the route is likely to be anything but straight. (978-1-60282-577-2)

Three Days by L.T. Marie. In a town like Vegas where anything can happen, Shawn and Dakota find that the stakes are love at all costs, and it's a gamble neither can afford to lose. (978-1-60282-569-7)

Swimming to Chicago by David-Matthew Barnes. As the lives of the adults around them unravel, high school students Alex and Robby form an unbreakable bond, vowing to do anything to stay together—even if it means leaving everything behind. (978-1-60282-572-7)

Hostage Moon by AJ Quinn. Hunter Roswell thought she had left her past behind, until a serial killer begins stalking her. Can FBI profiler Sara Wilder help her find her connection to the killer before he strikes on blood moon? (978-1-60282-568-0)

Erotica Exotica: Tales of Sex, Magic, and the Supernatural edited by Richard Labonté. Today's top gay erotica authors offer sexual thrills and perverse arousal, spooky chills, and magical orgasms in these stories exploring arcane mystery, supernatural seduction, and sex that haunts in a manner both weird and wondrous. (978-1-60282-570-3)

Blue by Russ Gregory. Matt and Thatcher find themselves in the crosshairs of a psychotic killer stalking gay men in the streets of Austin, and only a 103-year-old nursing home resident holds the key to solving the murders—but can she give up her secrets in time to save them? (978-1-60282-571-0)